SHOVEL NOSE AND THE GATOR GRABBERS

SHOVEL NOSE AND THE GATOR GRABBERS

ROBERT EDMOND ALTER

WILDSIDE PRESS

To Maritta Wolff.

Note: versions of the stories "Pig in a Poke," "Gator Grabbers," "Shoat Snatchers," "Shore-Fire Trap," "Dad's Day of Days," and "Dandy Deadfall" appeared in Boys' Life in 1959, 1960, 1961, 1962, and 1963.

PROLOGUE

In the beginning was the swamp. God made it and it took some doing. First the earth buckled under the sea, and mountains reached up, and land as soggy and porous as a wet sponge spread out, and then the sea drained back to its ocean basins and never returned again. The aquatic weeds and plants, abandoned in this abrupt manner, cast about desperately for substance and finally had to settle for the next best, the in-between of land and sea—the swamp.

One period followed another and each in turn brought something new—the arthropods, the amphibians, and all manner of little crawlies and growies, and the plants learned how to develop seeds and breed them on the wind and this reproduction created land food.

But who was to eat this food?

So, somewhere along here, God must have figured, "If you're going to have a huge soggy mess like this on your hands you might as well people it with something and get some use out of it." So He peopled the swamp with 'coons and wolves and minks, foxes and bears, rattlers and cottonmouths, and fish and birds. And, most important, gators.

A few million or so years later He created another critter for the swamp: a very special type of individual —a gator grabber called Dad Peps.

Now most of the swamp folk who knew Dad claimed that he never had been a baby or a boy or even a young man. No; they affirmed that Dad had been born as old as Methuselah, as cantankerous as Nero, and as greedy as Midas. Most folks, they said, had to grow up and learn how to become utterly worthless and slovenly and ignorant. But not Dad. He was that way from the word go.

Anyhow, Dad lived in Okefenokee with his Simple-Simon son Hughie, and they caught gators for a living. They were doing pretty well at it, too, until one day not so long ago....

Mama gator had set up a nursery for herself on a huge old hummock in an isolated lagoon. The place was stockaded by cocoplum surrounding red gumbo-limbo trees, wild coffee bushes and tamarinds all lacy with leaflets. In the center of this little island she had mashed down a clearing in the scrub and constructed her obtuse cone nest and, shortly, she had been delighted to behold one hundred and one ghastly little tads hatch out.

These gator tads were run-of-the-mill and nobody would have been able to distinguish one from another if it hadn't been for an accident that happened to one of the spidery-legged little critters one day. He had gotten into a fight with one of his brothers and in the hurly-burly of the battle they had overset a large rock which had landed heavily on the little fella's unformed snout, making it more shovel-nosed than nature had intended.

Unaware that his scooplike protuberance would instantly identify him for the remainder of his life, he had continued his carefree growing-up stage on the island with his brothers and sisters and his beautiful scut-plated, mud-daubed, knob-headed, toothy mama.

One day while Mama gator was out shopping for fish in the lagoon, the little scoop-nosed gator was frolicking on the shore of the hummock with a couple dozen of his brothers, when those two intrepid gator grabbers Dad and Hughie Peps came drifting quietly, cautiously around the bend in their grubby old skiff.

Old Dad chortled softly in his scraggly tobacco-stained beard.

"Hek! Hek! Looky thar, Hughie. Thet air islant's gator ground just like I thought. By grabbit, I bet thar be three-four more dozen a the li'l devils back in the bresh."

Hughie scratched at his thatch of colorless hair and looked blank.

"Well, what we-all want with li'l bitty gators, Dad? 'Tain't no use to us. Cain't sell 'em to nobody."

Dad clawed at his verminous beard and looked like he wanted to hit his witless son with something.

"Hughie, why is it a poor-joe bird got more sense in his inch-thick haid than you?" he wanted to know. "By juckies, boy, ain't you never goan larn *nuthin'* about gator grabbin'? You think you kin jest stand up an' say, 'Well, I'm goan go ketch me a gator to-day,' and tromp out and grab one jest like that?"

Dad spat a slim and accurate spurt of amber juice at a floating lily. He said:

"You got to know ahead a time *whar* to go! Whar to look! What to egg-spect when you git thar. Thet's what I'm a-doin' now—markin' this here site fer the future. Now I don't want you to fall overboard from surprise when I tell you this, but someday them air li'l tads is goan grow up to be great big rawly-pawly ga-tors. And thet's when I aim to git me some of 'em!" By this time the gator tads had spotted the skiff and the two humans and they started whining and yapping like a batch of ferocious wolf pups. They weren't about to be afraid of the two strange beings; on the contrary, they wanted to attack the Pepses.

"Lookit 'em, Hughie! Full a sand 'n vinegar, ain't they? Hey-day! Lookit thet li'l devil in front thar with his snout all upside down. Ain't he the feisty one? He's goan be a big daddy come a year er so!"

"Got him a nose like a shovel, don't he, Dad?"

"Hek! Hek! Thet's jest what he do, boy. Shovel Nose! Yessir! He's the one I'm aimin' my sights on." But Hughie's attention had wandered. He was casting uneasy glances around at the placid palm-boggy water.

"Dad, mebbe we best skedaddle. Them tads is kickin' up sech a ruckus a noise their ma might come rip-snortin' back any min-ute."

"I'll fix their noise fer 'em," Dad vowed, and he scooped up a handful of pebbles he had on the floorboards of the skiff and started pegging them among the irate little gators.

"*S'git*! You scut-haided li'l riptiles!"

The gator tads didn't go for the whizzing stones at all. They broke in a panic and went scrambling for the brush—all except the belligerent little fella with the shovel nose. He stood his ground and went *yap! yap! yap!* at the Pepses.

"Dad-blasted li'l lizard!" Dad fumed. "I'll git out an' kick his bent snout clean back to his scutty tail, is what. Don't he know who he be barkin' at?"

Hughie was getting so all-fired nervous it was all he could do to keep his skinny self still on the center thwart. He was looking right, left, and ahead with fearful expectancy.

"Dad! Dad! Never mind who he barkin' at. Let's haul out a here afore his ma—"

"I don't give a *blim-blam-blankity* about his four-leggit idjut ma!" Dad raged, reaching for more pebbles. "I'm pure-out goan larn thet shovel-nosed li'l fatmouth he cain't give Dad Peps no sass! I'm—"

Like a submarine surfacing and preparing to ram, Mama gator came up behind the stern of the skiff with a gurgling rush of breaking water and hitch-kicked her laterally compressed tail and charged full steam and good-gosh ahead.

"Look out!" Hughie yelled, and he grabbed for the stob pole, as Dad, tossing one pop-eyed look over his scrawny shoulder, snatched for his carbine.

Trouble was, Hughie was rattled and he wasn't watching what he was doing as he started to stand and he brought the butt end of the pole up on an angle just as Dad was ducking forward to grab the gun off the floorboards, and the end of the sturdy pole and the point of Dad's bearded chin made a beautiful *thop!* noise, the result of which spun Dad into a remarkable half-backward somersault, the carbine flying out of his hand and disappearing overboard as Dad came banging down in the stern among the litter of bait cans and fishing lines and gator-grabbing ropes, and *THH-PAMP!* Mama gator's blunt snout collided with the skiff.

It was a vivid moment, what with the momentum of the blow driving Dad's stern under the thwart and bringing his feet right on back to his ears as one of the glocky bait cans (full of fat, wiggly, slimy worms) upended over his head, and with Hughie's legs knocked clean out from under him as he dropped the stob pole overboard and toppled on top of Dad, and the helpless skiff scooting five yards ahead and, yay-hey! right smack into a log with a resounding *KA-RRRK!* Which opened the seams in the old skiff like sprung barrel staves. Which let all the gafocky swamp water in. Which started to flood the skiff. Which sank it.

Well, the things that Dad had to say as he stood in his skiff (which was now four foot underwater) with the drippy bait can cocked over his brow, can't be repeated, let alone printed, here or probably anywhere else. But it was rich, oh my yes, very rich indeed. And loud.

The essence of this bombastic speech had to do with the loss of the carbine, the stob pole, the bait cans (except for the one he was wearing), the fishing lines, and the gator-grabbing gear, not to forget the skiff.

And why had all these valuables been lost?

Dad knew very well why.…

Because of a little spidery-legged long-tailed fat-bodied scoop-snouted gator that stood on the marshy bank and still continued to yap-yap-yap at him.

That was the beginning of the legend of the gator grabber known as Dad Peps and the gator who would forever after be known as Shovel Nose.

CHAPTER 1

PIG IN A POKE

Shovel Nose waddled indignantly across a palm bog, pushing and rooting and pure-out smashing his way through the dense thin-stemmed undergrowth. He snorted repeatedly in vexation, and once let out a low rumble of anger. He had just been dispossessed and he was mad about it clear through and in no mood for nonsense.

An innocent tree frog, fresh from its hiding place and still a vivid green, *bar-rrumphed* at him majestically. Being an alligator, Shovel Nose's temper was of short duration, and now that he was a ten-foot gator he was accustomed to having his swamp passage undisputed. Quick as a wink his broad snout swung in a flashing arc and he snapped out of spite rather than hunger. But he was too late—the frog leaped back into its camouflage of leaves.

Just like that Shovel Nose forgot about the fat-mouthed tree frog and went on his waddling way. He had other worries. He didn't have what you might call intelligence, but he was endowed with a certain amount of memory plus a great deal of inherent instinct.

For example he knew Dad and Hughie when he saw them, and he knew from experience that they were out to get him; and that was only a part of his present troubles. His biggest problem at the moment was having been evicted from his personal pond by the giant bull gator that morning.

During the past two weeks Shovel Nose had been disturbingly aware of a she-gator who had taken abode in the first palmetto pond north of his. And on this particular bright, balmy, beautiful morning of spring he had left his cave in an unreasonably restless state. He had stood grandly in the shallows of his pond, inhaled deeply, and let out a terrific booming bellow. *BARRR-OOOM!* Thus announcing to all and sundry bull gators that he was going courting.

He had started out in fine waddling spirits, bedecked from paws to upper scuts with swamp mud, but was startled to discover—after a passage of only ten yards—that a great bull gator was already answering his challenge. The great gator was four yards long, four feet wide and half that thick. He had torn into Shovel Nose with a raging fury, pushing him back to his pond; and there—unwittingly accepting the axiom that retreat was the better part of valor—Shovel Nose had plunged into the slough and fled down the twisted waterway.

Later, when he had cautiously returned to reconnoiter (if not to reclaim) his pond, Shovel Nose had found the great gator contentedly sprawled on his own private mud-bank devouring a meal. It was only too plain to Shovel Nose that he must find himself a new home.

He tunneled through a thicket of amber berries, yellow jessamine, scarlet ivy trumpets and pink hurrah blossoms, approaching a sequestered pond with innate suspicion. It was a lonely secret place, landlocked with banks of black muck, thickets of tall tules, and huge clumps of palmettos. The gray mossbeard hanging in streamers from the cabbage palms stirred slightly. Nothing else moved. Sound was dead. Shovel Nose sniffed, turned his head from side to side, then waddled forward with confidence.

A young four-foot gator drifted from a weed bed, his bulbed eyes humping out of the water like two knots on a log. Shovel Nose chased him away quickly. He was in no mood to squabble over ownership of the pond.

Conqueror of all he could survey, Shovel Nose entered the water with a snort of righteousness. He nosed around his new property with a judicious eye, finally selecting a spot along the bank that was ornamented by the roots of a great tree. He went to work industriously.

He tore away the tangle of roots with his teeth, loosened the dirt with his shovel-like snout, then kicked the material behind him with his feet and swirled it into the water with his tail. He was pleased with his results. His cave was damp, dark, mucky and fetid. He snorted his satisfaction and nosed out into the water again.

He sank slowly to the bottom of the pond, his eye wary for a passing meal. A small school of amber-colored fish drifted his way. He froze, loglike, resting lightly on a bed of silt-covered rocks, and watched the fish through the transparent films that covered his eyes.

As the school finned leisurely toward him, Shovel Nose wadded up his tongue to close his throat. His jaws snapped open suddenly and, with a flick of his tail, his scutty body shot forward. His mouth was a natural fish basket. He swam back to his cave to enjoy his meal.

Minutes later he returned to the pond to scoop up and swallow a few small pebbles to help his digestion. Then he left the water to stretch out on the mud-bank and doze in the sun. Siesta time was his favorite time of day.

* * * *

The meaningless sound of men's voices startled him awake. He didn't pause to wonder or look. He knew what the voices meant. He scurried good-gosh along for the pond.

Once in the water he fled to the shelter of a maiden-cane bed; there he drifted, all but the tip of his snout and his eyes submerged, and pretended to be a log. A skiff was slowly working up the waterway to the pond, with Dad Peps sitting forward and Hughie standing aft poling.

"Hughie! Y'all gonna stop rockin' this here skiff? Or do I gotta step back an' wrap this rifle barrel about yer neck?"

"All I'm a-doin' is stobbin' like you tolt me, Dad! Y'all want me to git out an' push the stupid thing?"

If there was one thing Dad didn't want it was some free lip service from his worthless son.

"Want you to keep yer sassy-fyin' mouth shet, is what I want!" he yelled. "Easy…easy now…bring her leftward. Somethin' over yander an' it ain't no log. *Whoop!* Thar he be, boy! Thar's ol' Shovel Nose!"

The words meant nothing to Shovel Nose, nor did the sudden appearance of a rifle in Dad's hands; but the bow of the skiff turning abruptly toward the maiden canc brought the gator to instant action. He sucked a deep breath, closed his earflaps, shut off his nostrils, and sank hurriedly to the bottom. Somewhere above he heard the *KA-PLAM!* of the rifle.

He scurried across the mucky bottom, using the tips of his feet for locomotion, and rooted his way into another submerged reed bed. Then he surfaced slowly, snout first, for a little peek.

Dad and Hughie were some distance off in the boat. They were leaning over the gunwale inspecting the water. Dad looked mighty sour.

"Nope, I missed him," he grumbled. "Gun shy, thet's what he be. I seen 'em thetaway afore."

"Naw, he be skiff shy, Dad. Cain't no gator be gun shy. They ain't got them no brains a-tall—pore critters."

That was another thing Dad had no use for—Hughie telling *him* about gators.

"You ain't goan have much brains neither after I lay this here stob pole along yer ear. Arguefyin' with yer dad thetaway! Ifn I say he be gun shy, then thet's what he be! Now let's git stobbin' along here." Dad gave his scraggly beard a mean tugging, and his eyes flashed fiercely in his wicked old face.

"I tell you, Hughie, I'm a-goan git me thet big gator er somebody got to egg-splain to me why I ain't!"

Hughie wasn't quite as simple as he looked; he knew when not to give Dad an argument.

"I jest know thet you be, Dad. Thet's jest what I know."

The skiff drifted on down the waterway, and Shovel Nose, opening his great jaws, hissed wetly after it.

* * * *

In the late afternoon Shovel Nose swam quietly up the twistcd waterway, showing only the tip of his raised snout and the two knobs of his eyes, leaving practically no wake behind him.

A masked bandit squatting on a log washed its food in the water and eyed the gator suspiciously. At another time Shovel Nose might have considered an attempt to invite the raccoon to a one-sided dinner; but now he had more important things on his mind. He was going courting again.

The problem was twofold. He not only had to slip past the Pepses' shack, but past the great bull gator as well. He was more worried about the great gator than he was about Dad and Hughie. He took first things first. A pond with a waterway leading in and out lay before the Pepses' shack. Shovel Nose sank to the bottom and crossed it completely submerged. When the waterway petered out he emerged and started overland afoot.

He lumbered as carefully as possible through the palm bog. He knew that his old home—the great gator's pond—had no water exit. He would have to skirt his old domain by a wide margin in order to reach the she-gator's pond.

But just then a peculiar *choff-choff* noise came from the vicinity of the great gator's pond and Shovel Nose's curiosity conned him off course. He slid through a hurrah thicket slowly, his claws scrabbling on the dead leaves and twigs underfoot, and protruded the tip of his snout into the clearing.

The great gator was sprawled on a flat rock overlooking the pond. He was eating again and going at it with great gusto. Shovel Nose turned cautiously and waddled away. His scooplike lower jaw, turning up at the rear, suggested that he was smiling.

The she-gator lived on a small hummock island; a scaffolding of matted roots and silt, riddled with holes and teeming with insignificant crawly life. All in all, Shovel Nose thought it a superior piece of property to his other two holes.

He lumbered to a stop on the mud flat and let out a terrific bellow. It vibrated the boggy ground like an earthquake tremor. He could feel it running up through his feet and legs. The sensation pleased him.

The she-gator was lounging in the sun on her gaggly island. She turned her head slightly and opened one sleepy eye. They stared at each other expectantly.

"*Barrr-ooom!*" Shovel Nose said provocatively. He swished his great tail excitedly and waddled down to the water.

A pair of playful otters were waiting for him beneath the surface. They made quick fleeting passes at him, nipping at his feet and eyes, keeping well away from his dangerous tail. It was hopeless, he knew, to try to chase them in the green underwater world. They were far too adroit for him.

Peevishly, he slid into a submerged log litter where he knew they wouldn't dare follow, and settled down to wait. A moment or two passed and then the frolicking otters forgot about him completely. They scooted off into the emerald gloom to chase a water moccasin. Shovel Nose glided up from the bottom with grand unconcern, just as though the disgraceful incident had never occurred.

He lumbered heavily onto the bank and waddled toward the she-gator.

"*Barrr-ooom!*" he grumbled again, friendly-like.

The she-gator rolled languidly over on her back and waved her paws in the air. Her tail thrashed from side to side through the weeds. Shovel Nose pushed up to her and made short jabs at her white-plated belly with the tip of his snout. She snapped halfheartedly at his head. They were getting along fine, just fine.

"*BARRR-OOOM!*" A gigantic rumbling, earth-shaking, tree-quivering, leaf-loosening bellow shattered the courting scene.

The startled she-gator thrashed herself upright and lumbered hurriedly for the water. Shovel Nose turned expectantly, his tail flicking to and fro in anger. The great gator, agleam with swamp water and muck, was charging through the thicket at him.

Shovel Nose opened his mouth, emitting a sharp hiss, and went for his enemy with a short, fast lunge. They tangled, paws-mouths-tails, on the edge of the mud-bank. The great gator's tail swung heavily through the air and landed solidly against Shovel Nose's flank, sending him spinning into the brush, but he was right side up again as the great gator came at him with open, hissing mouth and he pulled back just as the great gator's toothy trap snapped at his throat. Then Shovel Nose lunged, snapping in turn, clamping his mouth about the other's jaws.

Unknowingly, Shovel Nose had stumbled upon the one big weakness in gator strength. When a gator's mouth is closed, the jaw muscles required to open it again are unbelievably weak. But now that he had his enemy practically helpless, he didn't know what to do with him. It was like catching a tiger by the tail.

Baffled, Shovel Nose resorted to savage habit. He jerked his head swiftly and violently, trying vainly to tear the great gator to bits. But the great gator's vast weight was far more than Shovel Nose could hope to manage. The scutty monster reared back, set his feet in the mud and refused to budge. He waited for Shovel Nose's hesitation, and then brought his tail into play again.

They spun, tearing through roots, brush and mud, like two spokes spinning on a wheel.

Shovel Nose was an old hand at mud-bank brawls. He knew when he was outclassed. He waited his time, picking it carefully— when they had both twisted over on their backs; then he released the great gator, wiggled hurriedly to his feet, and rushed madly for the water.

* * * *

Under the hushed spread of swamp twilight, Shovel Nose swam slowly homeward. He was a very discouraged gator.

He was restless that night. He thrashed about in his damp cave and made angry noises to himself. He was no longer satisfied with his new home. He wanted to live in the she-gator's pond with the she-gator. In his pea-sized brain he built a burning hate for the great gator; it even surpassed his hatred of Dad and Hughie.

A muted, distant knock of wood startled him. *Doomp!* He turned and slid noiselessly from his hide-hole into the black water, submerging all but his eyes. A light was hovering over the slough down by the maiden cane. It puzzled him because he vaguely remembered having seen its kind before, but he couldn't recall when. It was star-shaped and ruby red. It came closer.

"Thar he be, Dad! See his eyes a-burnin' like two fiery stars!"

A second light, larger and leaping, blared below the red star, and the fluttery quiet of the swamp exploded with a *KA-BALOWM!*

Shovel Nose felt something tear into the water along his flank as he dove hurriedly for the bottom.

Scrabbling through the water he looked up and saw the black shape of the skiff's bottom drifting over him. He elevated a couple of feet and gave the underside of the floorboards a sharp flip with his tail, spitefully. Then he scurried into the maiden cane and rose carefully to the surface. He could see the boat eight yards off, rocking dangerously, and Dad and Hughie clutching the gunwales. The red star rode on Dad's forehead. It was the night lamp he used for gator grabbing; the light invariably reflected in watchful gator eyes.

"Holt her! Holt her, doggone hit all! I purely got him thet time, boy! Thet was him a-thumpin' the keel in his death roll! Bet a purty he wallowed into thet water-lettuce bed yander to die. See hit move? See thar! Heyday! I've gone an' kilt ol' Shovel Nose! Hughie boy, y'all skip over the side with the stob pole an' root about in thar."

"You crazy er somethin'?" Hughie wanted to know. "I ain't *about* to go stompin' around in thet gafocky slough! Y'all want me to git my legs chawed offn?"

Dad did awful things to his beard, simply awful.

"Tell you jest what I want! Want you to stop all thet lippity-ness, you hear? I tell you I *got* him. You got nothin' to be scairt of. I'll cover you with the twelve-gage."

"*Twelve-gage!*" Hughie howled. "You'll blow the back a my ears around my nose with thet blame scatter gun! You flash a light-wood torch about in thar. I don't think you got him a-tall. An' I ain't fixin' to go at him till I know he be daid."

Dad, mumbling terrible things about his uncooperative son, leaned forward and removed a damp sack from the fire bucket they carried in the bow. He stirred the embers with a lightwood torch and held the wad of frying pitch aloft.

Shovel Nose watched the halo of flickering saffron light fall over the black pond; saw it pick up the vivid green of the water lettuce and turn the erect stalks of maiden cane into slim rods of gold.

"See thar, Dad? They ain't a speck a blood on the water. Nary a speck. And ain't no sign ner hair a ol' Shovel Nose neither. Reckon you gotta come agin hit—you jest pure-out din't git him."

Dad wasn't about to come "agin" it. And he said so too.

"I tell you *I cold got him!* I blew him snout-out-the-tail! And he's a-layin' down thar daid this minute!"

Hughie had to scoff. *Hek! Hek!* Which fetched him a clout over the head with the light wood torch from his slightly temperish parent.

"Dad! Dad! You silly ol' idjut! You want a set my haidbone afire?"

"Want you to hesh yer biggity mouth, is what I want!" Dad yelled. "Now hold the blim-blamity torch. I'm fixin' to git in thet air slough an' show you how gator grabbin' is done!"

Dad hopped overboard like a man who knew what he was doing. The inky water shot right up to his chest. "Hand me the pole," he ordered.

It was an opportunity that Shovel Nose had waited a long time for. He sank and gave a kick with his tail and skimmed forward like an arrow.

Dad shoved into the water lettuce and went jab-jab-jab at the muddy bottom with the stob pole. All at once the business end of the pole connected with an old dead cypress log.

"By juckies, what did I tolt you?" Dad crowed. "I've gone an' found him, is what. An' he's jest as cold daid as a pettyfied log!"

Shovel Nose cruised in alongside the skiff's starboard and pivoted himself about-face underwater. Then he rose gently to the surface and cocked his head and backrolled his left eye and raised his tail.

Hughie, his lower jaw dropping, watched the dripping tail rise alongside the skiff. "D-d-d-d-dad," he started to say.

"Shet up an' fetch me my gator-grabbin' rope," Dad commanded.

Chop-chop-chop! Shovel Nose's heavy tail gave Dad three fast heavy ones right on top of the cantankerous old fella's head, hammering him into the oozy bottom like a pile driver pounding home a stake.

"Hu-u-u-*EEE!*" Dad bellowed.

And Hughie got so rattled he dropped the gator-grabbing rope and snatched up the 12-gage, swinging the barrel on around, and cut loose without bothering about aim, target or anything, both barrels going *KA-BAL-LOWM!* and the recoil dumping him flat onto the floorboards, with Dad yelling:

"Hughie! You aimin' to blow my haidbone bald!"

It was a mighty battered, unhappy Dad that Hughie finally hauled into the skiff.

"By the horn-haided hoppin' hades I jest ain't goan settle fer hit! I ain't got me a gator skin all season and I'm goan git me *thet* one if I got a git me back in thet pond an' chase him *barehand*!"

But his heart wasn't really in it (or his head with the bumps, either). He sat down heavily and a moment later his voice drifted morosely across the swamp.

"Anybody kin catch him a little bitty gator; but do I catch me one the law goan whack me with a fat-type fine. They say I got to git me a *big* daddy like Shovel Nose. And Shovel Nose be the most uncatchin'est gator I ever see!" He shook his head mournfully.

"I don't know…sometimes I git to wonderin' why was I bornt in the swamp. Sometimes I git to wonderin' why I warn't bornt in the city an' be me a businessman er somethin' like."

"You ain't goan let one ol' gator git you down, air you, Dad?" Hughie worried. "You ain't goan let ol' Shovel Nose best you?"

Dad's spirit (and voice) snapped back with renewed vigor.

"Bust me if I be! Thinks he can keep dodgin' me, do he? Well, I'll larn Mr. Shovel Nose a thing er two. Thar ain't a gator livin' kin out-think me when I don't want 'em to!"

"Thet's the pay, Dad! Pitch hit to 'em! You bet they ain't. You the best gator out-thinker I ever seen."

"Shore I be!" Dad agreed. "Now pick up thet stob pole. Reckon we'll hustle back to the shanty whar I kin do me some thinkin' over a jug a cider."

"I jest know you goan beat ol' Shovel Nose, Dad. Thet's jest what I know."

Shovel Nose accompanied their departure with another wet hiss.

* * * *

In the early morning a fish eagle coasted down from the turquoise, cleared a green belt of maiden cane and made a tentative pass at something it saw in the water, then veered off sharply, leaving an expanding dimple on the dark surface. It winged high over Shovel Nose and banked for the cypress barrier.

The gator followed the bird's flight for a moment, then he eased himself into the sheltering green shade of a palmetto stand. He was scouting the activity of the two gator grabbers.

Dad and Hughie had cleared a small circular section of shrubbery between the great gator's pond and Shovel Nose's new pond, and were now driving a deep stake into the damp earth in the very center of the clearing. Next, from a boxed cage, they fetched a young squealing piglet and harnessed it to the stake. Then they stood back and admired their work (Hughie's work, actually; Dad was best at giving directions and fatherly advice).

"Wait till ol' Shovel Nose cuts acrost this here porker. He shore gonna pause a bit to gorge hisself. Hek! Hek! An' I goan be up in thet air tree yander a-waitin' fer him!" Dad rubbed his hands in anticipation. "Reckon he must got him a she-gator somewhars about here, else he wouldn't be doin' him so much trompin' from pond to pond."

"Thet shore out-thinks anythin' I ever see, Dad," Hughie said admiringly. "You ort a been a gen'ral. Reckon when porker spies ol' Shovel Nose he'll purely raise a ruckus. We kin crawl off in the brush an' have us a snooze. All thet squealin' will wake us sharp."

Shovel Nose backed off a bit and started north. The piglet had looked mighty inviting, but Shovel Nose didn't trust Dad and Hughie. He liked a tasty meal as well as the next gator, but right now he had the she-gator on his small mind.

He followed the short twisted path through the thicket down to the great gator's pond. His enemy was lying peacefully on the mud-bank, his jaws choff-choffing, still eating.

Shovel Nose planted his stubby legs firmly in the oozy turf, sucked air into his lungs and let out a BARRR-OOOM! that brought all kinds of little crawly life frantically from their trembling earth apartments. Instantly the great gator was all action. His head snapped up, his tail lashed furiously. He turned with lightning speed, spotted Shovel Nose and emitted an angry hiss. He charged with wide-open mouth.

Shovel Nose spun around quickly and lumbered back up the path. He could hear the great gator's claws scrabbling over the leaves and twigs close behind him but he didn't worry about it. He knew from experience that he could outrun the monster.

He veered sharply to the south and thundered straight for the palm bog he had recently vacated. Plowing through fronds, reeds, mossbeard and catclaw he emerged in the clearing. The piglet took one look and shrank back and then made a short-lived dash to the end of its leash and began squealing hysterically.

Shovel Nose's short stumpy legs chopped at the turf as he blundered across the clearing and he whooshed right by the piglet without even bothering to turn his head. Somewhere to his right he heard Dad's voice shouting about something.

He charged the screen of brush, his blunt snout driving like a wedge, leaving in his wake the frantic squealing of the piglet and the sudden chest-deep grunt of surprise from the great gator as *he* spotted the little fat tasty.

Without warning, Hughie sprang up all pop-eyed before Shovel Nose's charge and yelled in terror.

"*WHAA!* Holt on thar!"

Shovel Nose pivoted the hind portion of his scutellated body, sweeping his powerful tail through the weeds like a scythe, whisking Hughie's legs out from under him and leaving him in a rifle-over-boy heap. He straightened his four-legged course and lumbered northward.

"*Great day in the mawnin'!*" Dad roared. "Hughie! Looky here at the size a the one chasin' ol' Shovel Nose!"

Dad cut loose with both barrels. *KA-BLAM-BLAM!*

"Hugh-*EEE!* He's makin' off with our pig! Git him, boy! Pump hit to him, Hughie! I got to reload!"

But he chose the wrong place and time to do it—just at the edge of the clearing and right in the great gator's path. The monster charged him with his mouth full of unhappy pig, and he went through Dad like a bowling ball making a one-pin spare: Dad's twelve-gage and shells going one way high in the air and Dad going another, and Dad beating them down to the ground and landing as heavily as a gunny sack full of bricks.

"Hu-hu-*hughie!* Why ain't you shootin' him? You simple-haided—"

"Thet's jest what I'm a-tryin' to do, dang-whack hit all! Ol' Shovel Nose cold near to crippled me! Thet's what he done!"

"Never mind about that! Hurry, you blame fool of a boy! Cut thet big riptile off from the water! Run him east, Hughie! *East!* You consarn witless stumblin' idjut! Pump hit to him! By grabbit, I never in all my bornt days seen sech a gator!"

"I'm a-doin' the dang-whackedest best I kin fer a boy with two broke legs! Why don't *you* do somethin', 'stead a runnin' off at the mouth!"

"I ain't got time for no sassifyin'. You hop along thar with thet rifle! I goan chase thet pig-stealin' gator clean out a Okefenokee ifn I got to…"

Shovel Nose paused on his path and raised his head to listen to the diminishing sound of the distant confusion. Then he grunted his satisfaction and started on his way again for the she-gator's pond.

His snooplike lower jaw, turning up at the rear, suggested that he was grinning.

CHAPTER 2

THE GATOR GRABBERS

Hughie was leaning his long pipestem body out the shanty window, watching a bump of movement that was traveling against the sluggish current of Crick Crack Creek. He was certain that the moving bump was Shovel Nose—or rather, the very tip of the gator's bent snout. Without doubt Shovel Nose was trying to sneak past the shanty, heading upstream to his pond. Hughie's hand itched for his rifle.

"Dad," he called, "I reckon you must be pure-out sick."

Dad, sitting at the table with his cider jug and his smoke-spluttering corncob, put a skinny claw of a hand into his snarly beard and glared at Hughie peevishly.

"Why at do you say thet?" he wanted to know.

Hughie pulled himself in from the window.

"'Cause you ain't been an' took a shot at ol' Shovel Nose in a week, is why. Thet jest ain't like you, Dad."

Dad snorted, as if to say, *How kin a man have seek a fool fer a son?*

"Hughie, when the Lord said *Brains*, you must a thought He said *Trains*, and you plain missed yours. I ain't takin' me a shot at him 'cause I don't want him daid, is why."

Hughie was aghast. "Don't want him daid? Since when?"

"Since I found out they ain't enough money in gator hides. The business these days is in live gators. Them air tourist-type centers pay top money fer live gators to use fer display. And, Hughie, thet's what I'm fixin' to do with Shovel Nose. You'n me is goan do us some real gator-grabbin'!"

"Real gator-grabbin'? How do we go at thet, Dad?"

"You'll see, boy, you'll see. Hek! Hek!"

Being an alligator. Shovel Nose was not given to prolonged reasoning; but being an animal of the vertebrata classification he was subject to habit-conditioning. Do a thing consistently, long enough, and the gator's brain would recognize a pattern. And that's why Shovel Nose was worried. Dad and Hughie had broken their pattern, had stopped chasing him with their skiff and guns.

He wended his way cautiously up the twisted waterway that meandered along the foot of the Pepses' shanty, riffling the surface gently with the tip of his asymmetrical snout, snorffing the fetid air suspiciously.

Twice during the past week, while engaged in his favorite occupation—floating on the surface, pretending to be a log, looking for fish or a water turkey—he'd almost bumped into Dad's skiff. Both times he'd looked up in startled fear to see Dad sitting there staring down at him with evil-eyed speculation. Each time he'd thrashed frantically for the bottom of the slough, and each time Dad hadn't made a move to stop him. That just wasn't like Dad Peps. Shovel Nose didn't understand it; and what he didn't understand he didn't like.

He submerged the tip of his snout and sank his entire length to a horizontal position. Through the protective films that covered his eyes he stared at the turquoise underwater world. As a general rule he had five simple emotion gears: he was either hungry, sleepy, curious, frightened, or temperish. Right now he was temperish.

A fat water moccasin twisted toward him, forming S-shapes in the water. When the cottonmouth bumped snouts with the drifting gator it recoiled with a silent snap and shot off into the color-spectrum. Shovel Nose slammed his jaws in a vicious bite and was rewarded with a mouthful of water. He snorfled furiously and lashed his armored tail spitefully.

He hung suspended in the slough for a long moment, glaring about to see if anything else was going to give him a bad time. Nothing did. He snorted again and propelled himself upstream with his tail.

There was more than just Dad's sudden inconsistency that made Shovel Nose temperish: there was also the loss of his private sunbank.

The sunbank was a sequestered spot off from the main waterway. It was surrounded on three sides by tupelo and titi and it fronted a small brackish pond. But its best feature was the fact that it was inaccessible to men in a skiff. Its fourth side was a tall thick wall of maiden cane. Shovel Nose could thrash overland through the palm bog and into the hide-hole and doze in the sun all day without fear of Dad and Hughie sneaking up on him.

But recently the high land directly behind his hide-hole had been invaded by a horde of mama gators. The grass and reeds had been beaten down for half an acre around and the expectant mamas had proceeded to build a gator-nest somewhat on the pattern of an encampment.

With mud and grass they'd constructed a series of obtuse cones four feet high and four feet diameter at the base. On a floor of mortar they had deposited a layer of eggs, covered the eggs with more mortar, laid another layer of eggs, covered it, and so on up to the top of the huts.

At about hatching time Shovel Nose's curiosity had foolishly prompted him to go investigate the nest. He'd blundered through the tules in a more or less affable mood, snorfling and grunting, and waddle-legged it toward the nearest cone hut. Instantly the challenging *baarumphs*, the bellowings and roarings of the outraged mamas, had shattered the peaceful swamp stillness like the advent of a thunderstorm.

They had hit him from four directions at once, giving it to him with teeth, tails, paws and massive body weight. Shovel Nose had fled ingloriously from his private sunbank, nor had he been back since.

The sun was high over the titi, cypress and cabbage palms, double-sized and white like a hot branding iron, when Shovel Nose approached the pond he considered home. His sun-basking time was long overdue. He couldn't stay awake any longer. He headed in to shore.

A deer, its front feet in the water, velvetlike antlers up, blinked at him with liquid eyes, then bolted for the thicket. Shovel Nose ignored the frightened buck. He lumbered ashore, turned himself nose-to-the-water (just in case) and settled down on his leather-plated belly on the warm sand.

Sleep wasn't far off…it rolled lightly over his body and tumbled into his eyes.

* * * *

The skiff came slow and quiet, leaving an almost imperceptible wake on the bright emerald water, pushing cautiously through the bonnets alongside, whispering them. Hughie stood aft stobbing with the pole. Dad sat forward, his 12-gage handy between his legs, a long coil of rope—noosed at the business end—in his lap.

"Easy—easy now, you thinkless excuse fer a human bean," he cautioned softly in his peevish manner.

"I'm stobbin' so easy I might as well be usin' me a toothpick 'stead a this here pole," Hughie muttered back.

"Might as well be usin' you a brain 'stead of thet mouth a yorn," Dad snapped angrily, forgetting his own warning. Then he hush-hushed Hughie, as though the boy and not himself had made all the noise. A moment later he started whispering frantically.

"See him! See him a-sleepin' hisself silly thar? *Leftward*, Hughie. Come leftward likn I tell you!"

Dad set his 12-gage aside and began stretching out the noosed rope. Hughie watched the occupation with a dour eye.

"Wisht we could jest cold blast away atn him, Dad. You shore gosh ain't goan git you a prettier shot than thet air one."

"Goan take me a shot at thet big gate-type mouth a yorn ifn you don't hesh when I tell you! We goan take us ol' Shovel Nose alive. Now *eeee-asy*, Hughie…*HUGHIE!* Lord a li'l jaybirds, boy! Will yer look out thar fer thet breather!"

The "breather," a gnarled cypress knee jutting from the water, seemed to spring magically at the bow of the skiff under Hughie's inept steering. The skiff and the knee collided with a hollow *tuunk!*

Right now Shovel Nose was awake and he opened his eyes and started up, seeing the skiff only one yard away from his snout and seeing Dad reaching out with the noose.

But in their impetuous haste to capture Shovel Nose, Dad and Hughie had forgotten a safety rule in gator-grabbing: *Never cut a gator off from the water.* Shovel Nose saw the skiff and the two men between himself and the slough and he went witless with fear. He charged straight into the side of the skiff as the noose dropped over his protruding head.

KA-SLAM! Gator and skiff came together; gator dove dizzily underwater; skiff stood straight up on its side. Then the rope wrapped hard about the elevated gunwale and the underside of the skiff, snagging the diving gator, and he jerked into a halt and began to thrash.

Things were precarious topside. The skiff was standing on its port beam, with Hughie standing on one foot on the raised gunwale, the other wagging in the air, as he clung most of his weight to the end of the stob pole which was bending farther and farther away from the skiff, while Dad had both feet braced against the canted floorboards, leaning his body back into an almost horizontal position to the water, holding hard to the rope that was still wrapped around and under the boat.

"I got him, Hughie! I shore gosh got him this time! Lend a hand here, you tom-fool of a boy! Hep your dad haul him in!"

"Haul him in?" Hughie bellowed. *"He's haulin' us in!"*

Which was no under- or over-statement. Shovel Nose, not able to understand why he couldn't swim clear, finally decided that it had something to do with the hated skiff over his head. So, blind with panic, he attacked the boat, coming up under the submerged gunwale with his great corrugated back…which was all that the skiff needed.

The craft buckled high in the water and Hughie let out a shout as it skittered away from him, leaving him hanging on the bending stob pole with nothing under him but churned swamp water, as Dad spun ankles-over-appetite, twisting himself in the coils of leaping rope, caromed once on the water like a skipping cannon ball, banged *WHAP!* into the cypress knee (also like a cannon ball), and sank. Straight down.

Shovel Nose's panic was now complete. Overhead the skiff was slewing around like something gone crazy, then the stob pole broke and Hughie came crashing underwater with all the bait cans and whatnot, and still the poor gator had the rope secured about his snout with Dad's weight lashed to the far end.

Enough was enough. Shovel Nose took off for a distant reed bed, hauling and twisting bubble-mouthed helpless Dad after him, smacking him into "breathers," rebounding him off submerged logs, tugging him through maiden cane and golden-heart lilies and pick-erelweed…until finally the line snapped and Dad wobbled to the surface.

It was a bedraggled, soggy, half-drowned Dad that Hughie hauled out of the water and onto the mud-bank. First off, Dad spat out a lily, then he unswallowed maybe a quart of brackish swamp water, then he did some spluttering and gasping, and after that he chased himself through the shallows until he found his pulpy old hat.

Hughie thought that Dad merely wanted to save the hopeless old relic (Lord knows why), but it wasn't so. Dad came ashore, threw the hat *splok!* in the mud and then began jumping up and down on it, both feet at once. *Thomp-thomp-thomp!* And finally he found his voice.

"By the cross-eyed Katie, I ain't a-gonna have hit! Now *I tell yer!* Shovel Nose has pure-out gone and done it this a-time! Thet blim-blam-blankity gator has gone and got him my dander! I'm a-goan tear wildcats apart withn my teeth! I'm a-goan take cottonmouths an' wrop 'em about my middle fer belts! I'm a-goan rip up cypress trees and use 'em fer clubs! I'm a roarin' brawlin' glass doorknob-chewin' cadaver-maker from Okefenokee! I'm a-goan cotch him and I'm a-goan beat him and hit him and kick him and I'm a-goan do him a hurt till he be black 'n blue! Now you *hear me*, Hughie!"

Hughie *did* hear him—half the swamp heard him. Hughie cried:

"Thet's it, Dad! Whale hit to him! Beat him silly! I know you, Dad. When yer dander be up, why they ain't nothin' on earth kin stop you from bargin' smack ahead!"

* * * *

Fifteen minutes later Shovel Nose poked his knobby eyes above the water and watched the two gator grabbers paddle away in their half-swamped skiff. He gave them a wet hiss of indignation and turned for shore.

But he was worried. He couldn't understand what Dad and Hughie had been trying to do. The new tactics kept nudging a spark of warning in his small brain. Something more was going to happen. His inherent instinct, that reached way back to his dim ancestor the Eryops, told him that something more was coming.

Without actually reaching a conscious decision the gator nosed into a sandbank like a landing craft and waddled from the water. Far off, a lone limpkin wailed its lost-child cry and an osprey cleared the tall wall of cypress and sycamore and hit the sky as though it had been thrown there. Further up the creek something went *sploop* in the water but the sound was too far off and minor to concern Shovel Nose. He listened to the *burrumf* of the bullfrogs and the sudden low whine of a hunting panther, and started inland. Everything was normal. Safe—for the moment.

He scrabbled through the tules, pin-downs and hurrah bushes, detoured a petrified log litter, nosed across a shallow pond and entered a palmetto grove. Instinct guided him like a built-in radar set straight to his hidden sunbank. But first he must skirt the gator-nest.

He slid craftily into a tupelo thicket, warily eying the cone huts, and scurried for the swollen bole of a solitary cypress. He was almost home. And then he startled a poor-joe bird that had been pecking at the dead leaves for tasty tidbits. The poor joe rose in agitation, squawling indignantly at Shovel Nose.

Instantly there swept from the huts a myriad of little foot-long gators, all yipping and yapping like small pups. To the startled observer they would appear to be six inches of mouth and teeth, and six inches of tail. And all twelve inches of them was voracious courage. On their crooked little spider legs, they came after Shovel Nose with a fury that was nightmarish.

In his consternation Shovel Nose forgot that the sturdy cypress was towering right before him. He turned hurriedly and banged his snout against the bole and that set him back a bit. He paused, blinking foolishly, as the gator pups swarmed all around his scutted flanks, yipping, twisting, snapping. Then he heard the sound he feared even more than the blast of Dad's gun.

"*BARRR-OOOM!*"

The outraged horde of amazon mama gators came charging from the tules with their huge hissing mouths wide open. With one horizontal sweep of his tail Shovel Nose bowled over thirty of their devilish little offspring, and took off at a full-bodied run straight for a jungle wall of many colors. Smashing and clawing, he hit the bright tapestry of yellow jessamine and scarlet ivy trumpets and pink hurrahs, and broke through and lumbered out onto his private sunbank—which was no longer private. The gator pack was hot on his tail.

Shovel Nose struck the water like a log coming down a chute and tail-kicked his way across the pond to the morass of maiden cane. He had a frantic few moments in there, getting himself hung up on the jutting cane-ends, on the knobby cypress knees, on the crisscrossed dead logs, and when he tried to veer to the right and gain the high ground of a hummock, a honey bear-working the larvae in a rotten tree—vexatiously gave him a paw-bapping on the top of his humpy head.

Shovel Nose cleared the cane and plowed limply into the broad slough on the far side. He sucked a hasseling breath into his lungs, closed his earflaps, shut off his nostrils and sank like a mossy old boulder to the murky bottom. He was beaten and he knew it. He didn't need instinct to tell him so.

* * * *

In the afternoon, while Shovel Nose was sleeping unhappily in his cave—a small dark hole in the creek bank—those two intrepid gator grabbers, Dad and Hughie, came slogging across the palm bog on foot. Along with a spade, Dad was carrying a fresh coil of rope. Hughie carried the shotgun. They'd moored their skiff around the bend and had hoped to sneak up on Shovel Nose in his hole, but unwittingly they had stumbled into the gator-nest.

Again the gator *barrr-oooms* tore up the fabric of the swamp silence, and again the outraged gators swarmed out to chase any and all invaders from the nursery.

Dad (the roarin' brawlin' cadaver-maker who was going to tear wildcats apart with his teeth) quickly legged it for the nearest cabbage palm to show Hughie how fast he could shinny up the bole. Hughie, however, turned and cut loose with both barrels of the 12-gage and the mama gators and their tads, startled by this unexpected development, fled in a great scrabbling clump for the tupelo.

"Hi, Dad!" Hughie crowed. "Looky thar what I went an' done!"

"Probably went and scairt Shovel Nose smack back into the slough!" Dad yelled, coming down from his tree. "Hurry up, afore he gits away!"

Shovel Nose was jolted awake by the gunfire but he had no idea what was happening. He knew, however, that it meant that Dad and Hughie were back. He started to leave his hole, but— too late. He heard the *thup-thup-thup* of their footsteps pounding overhead. He cowered back into the darkness, playing possum.

"By juckies, Hughie! Right under our feet is ol' Shovel Nose's hide-hole. I know, 'cause I been spyin' on him all week. And *you* thet thought I was gittin' soft 'n sick in the haid!"

"Well, I pure-out got to hand hit to you, Dad. You went and out-foxed ol' Shovel Nose as shore's mud's soft. But what I cain't git in my brainbox is *how* we to git him outn thar now thet we gone cotched him?"

Dad had to chuckle. "Hek! Hek! Hughie, ifn you had you some brains in thet box you speak of, 'stead a jest hot air floatin' about in thar, you *might* larn you a somethin'. Now, boy, you jest fetch me some long clean thick sticks. Yer dad is goan larn you some *ree*-al gator-grabbin'!"

Shovel Nose didn't know what to make of all the activity. He thought that by keeping still and out of sight Dad and Hughie wouldn't know he was there. When the first thick stake came driving down through the den entrance he stared at it blankly and hunched back in his hole. Then the second came and the third, and then he woke up…again too late. He was trapped.

"Now, Hughie boy, you start spadin' off the roof of thet hole. See the trick? We tear off the top an' we cold got him in a box! All we got to do then is drap the noose around him and git a cinch on his jaws. Cain't no gator in the world hurt a body when his jaws is tied."

"'Ceptin' with his tail, Dad. Don't go fer to fergit his tail."

"I ain't fergittin' hit. Ifn he goes to git sassy with me, I'll tie him around a tupelo with'n it, thet's what! Git spadin'."

Shovel Nose moved back and forth nervously in his tight quarters, grumbling to himself as the dirt came pouring down on his scutted back and head, and finally he snapped at it spitefully. His temper was growing short, mighty mighty short.

Suddenly he saw bright clean light overhead and he couldn't understand how it came there and minutes later, as the hole expanded, he saw Dad and Hughie peering down on him and he knew he was in for very serious trouble.

"Thar he be!" Dad cried. "Thar be the consarn leg-bustin' skiff-smashin' riptile! Easy on with the noose, Hughie. I'll cover you with the twelve-gage."

Which didn't suit Hughie at all.

"But Dad—why cain't I cover *you* with the gun? *You* be the gator grabber here. I'm jest larnin'."

"Hughie, you melon-haided excuse fer a boy! Air you goan stand thar argufyin' with yer dad when Shovel Nose is on'y three feet away an' jest a-beggin' to be caught? Git thet noose a-movin', else I'll *move you* with the butt of this here gun!"

Hughie, muttering one or two observations about his loving dad, slowly lowered the noose into the pit and Shovel Nose made a hissing snap at it, but Hughie jerked it aside, and then—before the gator could get his ponderous jaws open again—he whipped the noose around the concave snout and cinched the line taut.

Shovel Nose thrashed his body frantically from side to side, snorting through his nostrils and scrabbling the mud of his den with his horny paws, but he couldn't free his jaws. He was baffled; couldn't understand what had happened to him. Then his sense of self-preservation shouted for escape to the water and he started scrambling up the sloping side of the pit.

Dad was dancing about in a wild circle. "Holt him, Hughie! Now he's a-comin' fine! Wait till I git the other end a the rope an' wrop hit around his hindquarters!"

"Mind his tail, Dad… *DAD!* You ain't a-mindin' his—"

Shovel Nose took a wide vicious cut at Dad's brittle legs with his armored tail, and for the second time that day Dad went off in a roly-poly somersault. This time he ended up on his face in the mud at the bottom of the gator hole, and for fifteen seconds you couldn't hear the appalling words he was saying because of all that glocky muck in his mouth.

Shovel Nose was confused. In his panic to escape, he started off in the wrong direction, going away from the water and dragging Hughie after him.

"Hep me, Dad! Hep me! He be gittin' away!"

Dad came up sputtering clots of mud. "No, he ain't! He's headin' him the *wrong* way! Stay with him, boy! He cain't do nuthin' with his jaws tied! I think he gone busted my legs, is what!"

Shovel Nose charged blindly into a pin-down thicket and that was the end for Hughie.

The hurrah bushes are one thing. They are tall and thick and pesky, but a man can put up with them if he has it to do. But nobody in his right mind has any use for pin-downs. The Adam stalk grows out of water and its branches loop over and take root in the soggy ground, forming hoop snares for feet, and those roots grow new stalks with branches which also bend down and take root and the whole affair goes on like that for acres, hoop after hoop hoop hoop.

Hughie had himself ankle-twisted and leg-tangled and tripped flat within ten feet. He dropped the rope.

Still, things were not rosy for Shovel Nose. With his jaws strapped he was defenseless. He blundered head-on into a cypress knee and a sharp jutting branch ran under his long chin, under the noose. He twisted to and fro, whipping his great body about like a pendulum gone mad. He was hooked tight.

Hughie came racing back for the 12-gage and Dad started yelling.

"Hughie! Don't shoot him, you sap-brained idjut! I want him *alive!* Jest *tone him down* a bit, boy!"

The sharp branch sawed through the noose like a dull knife, and for a moment Shovel Nose continued to churn up the peaty earth without realizing he was actually free. It was that very moment that Hughie approached him from behind, gripping the 12-gage by the barrel.

Hughie's idea of "toning" Shovel Nose was to give him three *Bop! Bop! Bops!* on top of the head with the gun butt. Shovel Nose went blink-blink-blink, then looked back at Hughie and started grinning his gator grin.

Hughie couldn't believe the bad news. He looked at the yawning maw of mouth, at the beefy wedge of tongue, at the irregular rows of white teeth—each like a stob pole—and decided that he'd had it as a gator grabber.

"*DAD!* His gafocky jaw be open!"

Hughie dropped the gun and went legging it back through the pin-downs, and Shovel Nose let loose an earth-trembling roar of rage and started after him. And, all in all, it wasn't the best news in the world for Dad, either. He saw Hughie coming, saw an open-mouthed Shovel Nose coming after him, and decided that his legs weren't broken after all. No sir, by grabbit! He came from the hole like a jack-in-a-box, cleared the edge of the bank in one Tarzan-like leap, and went hot-footing along the shore.

But talk about *speed!* Hughie passed Dad as though the old fool were standing still. They went smashing through the hurrahs and titi, tripping and stumbling and lurching over the hoop bushes and through the cane and the blim-blam choke-berry and the eye-snagging catclaw and shin-banging log litter; and all the while the mama gators and their tads stood back in the tupelo thicket and watched the remarkable chase in silent wonder.

Hughie reached the skiff first and you would have thought he was on his way to a gold strike—lunging his shoulder against the stern and shoving the craft into the bonnets and pickerelweed and heaving himself over the gunwale any way he could and snatching for the pole.

Dad came thrashing into the shallows after him, his feet and legs spinning up the water like Catherine wheels, with Shovel Nose right at his shirttail and snapping his toothy jaws like two manhole covers slamming together.

"Wait fer yer dad! *Wait!* You empty barrel-haided idjut!"

"Wait *nuthin'!*" Hughie yelled. "If you comin' with me, you best have you some wings! 'Cause I'm fixin' to *fly!*"

He began stobbing with the pole like a man churning butter in a bucket, and that's the way they went down the creek—Hughie gouging out the bottom of the slough, and Dad hanging to the stern and still kicking up great thrashings of water and still announcing to all the inhabitants of the swamp what a worthless boy Hughie was.

Shovel Nose stood with his forefeet in the water, watching the frantic retreat of the two gator grabbers. Then he snorfled his contempt and turned back for the palm bog. The mama gators and their tads were returning to the nest. Shovel Nose half expected them to attack him. But they didn't. They watched him with a bright light in their round humped eyes.

He waddled through the tupelo and down to his private sunbank. There was still some sun left in the sky, enough to sleep comfortably in for an hour or so. Everything considered, it had been a pretty good day.

CHAPTER 3

THE SHOAT SNATCHERS

Shovel Nose was all big-eyed in the maiden cane. Any sudden noise in the swamp always startled him, and right now the noise around the Widow Harks' shanty was worse than a good-gosh flock of green-winged teal passing overhead.

He had been basking himself on a nearby sandbank when the ruckus started, and his first waking reaction had been for flight. Off he'd gone, lumbering for the water like a fat man waddling for the dinner table, and then into the nearest hummock of maiden cane. And now, snug in his nest, he was peering through the reeds with a curiosity that would put a cat to shame.

The Widow Harks was a tall rawboned woman with a face as pleasant as a Comanche Indian's on a war party. She was standing in her yard with both hands wrapped about a broom handle and with the business-end of the broom poised over her right shoulder, and any fool could see that she was in no mood to pass the time of day with a neighbor.

Directly in front of her was Dad Peps, and his scraggly old beard was purely a-quiver with agitation. Hughie, not being quite as simple as Dad made out, had diplomatically removed himself from the vicinity of the widow's broom and was perched some twenty feet off on top of a split-rail fence. But Dad was never one to retreat from a disputed position without full decorum, broom or no broom.

"I done tolt you afore and I'm cold tellin' you fer the last time," the widow screeched with a voice like a clawed bobcat's in a fight, "to keep shed of my property! *Trass*-passin', thet's what yer a-doin'! *Trass*-passin'!"

"'Tain't so! 'Tain't so!" Dad cried defensively. "Me 'n Hughie was jest passin' through to home, is all. How in the name a li'l green turtles is Hughie 'n me to git home ifn we don't come by here?"

"You kin go along the crick in yer skiff like t'other folk do, is how!" the Widow Harks kindly informed him. "You don't go to pull no wool over my eyes, Dad Peps. You'n yer no-account simple-minded excuse fer a son done cut acrost my backyard so's you could eyeball my shoat pen!"

Dad opened his mouth but he didn't stand a chance. For once in his bombastic life he was outclassed.

"I done lost me two a my shoats in the past two months," the widow war-whooped, "and I ain't fixin' to lose me no more! Now I ain't namin' no names, but if I miss jest *one* more shoat I'm goan shoot me a raggedy old man with a once-white beard!"

Now Dad was a raggedy old man and his beard might have been white once upon a time, though ever since Hughie had known him it had been an unkempt tobacco-stained (*Guk!*) affair of a definite yellowish hue. But Dad was quick and he got the point.

"You cain't go to call me no shoat-snatcher, you old scarecrow in skirts!" he bellowed, and he turned his head (which was his second mistake for the day) toward the split-rail.

"Hughie, you heered what this clock-stoppin' old biddy went and callt me?"

WHAMP! Dad caught the business-end of the broom across the back of his neck, and he jolted a step forward like a man bending down to see if his shoes need tying, with his eyes popping like stepped-on grapes, as Hughie cried:

"Look out, Dad! She's fixin' to pound y'all!" (Big news.)

And Dad opened his mouth to say, "Well, don't jest set thar like a frog on a log," when—*WHUNK!* the broom came from the other direction and slammed him flush in the face and his words were all lost in whiskers and broom straws.

Dad wasn't completely foolish; he knew when the time for decorum was long gone. He got his spindly shanks underway and started legging it for the fence. But the Widow Harks went broom-swinging right after him. *WHAMP-WHAMP-WHAMP!* on top of

Dad's head. And Dad hit that fence like a bear going up a tree after honey, and Hughie got in a panic and tried to jump clear but his legs were crossed under the top rail and he lost his balance and went topsy-turvey into the weed, and the Widow Harks leaned over the fence and gave him two good licks as well.

Shovel Nose watched the two gator grabbers go thrashing off through the tupelo and he snorffed a snort of contentment. He was such a big hard-scutted gator that there really wasn't much in the swamp to frighten him—except Dad and Hughie. But now that they were gone he could relax and pick up his serene afternoon where he'd left it, before Dad had come along with his fat mouth.

He drifted out of the maiden cane and tail-kicked his way back to shore. Grunting and snorfing he hauled his great dripping-wet bulk out of the water and onto the bank. Then, with an eye for comfort, he selected a long dead cypress log and crawled on top of it and sprawled out for his siesta, legs hanging down on either side.

A cooter bird, all duck-footed and beady-eyed, ambled along the far end of the log, and nearby in the slough a young gator started grunting-up for attention; but Shovel Nose ignored sights and sounds. Overhead the sun was white-fire hot and a thick sleepy silence settled over the swamp without a hitch. Shovel Nose closed his eyes and pictured the Widow Harks' plump little shoats in his mind. Also in his stomach.

He'd had his eye on the pigpen in the widow's backyard for some time now, and the temptation of a fat pig dinner was slowly becoming an obsession in his small brain. But instinct wouldn't allow him to hang around the pigpen in broad daylight. Moonlit night was shoat time—sultry afternoons were for napping.

But he reckoned without the Widow Harks' touchy temper.

She spotted him down there on the log as she was heading back to her shanty and she made a stormy detour to the top of the sandbank.

Shovel Nose's sun-basking shoat dreams came to an abrupt end as the first rock went *thomp!* on his flat head. His eyes popped open and automatically he started unhinging his great jaws in order to give someone or something a good bite, and right now the

Widow Harks' voice whipped at him like the furious snap of a cottonmouth.

"Ifn you think I'm goan have me a shovel-faced riptile a-loa-fin' about my property, jest a-waitin' to pick off one a my prize shoats like thet Dad Peps, then you pure-out got you another think comin'! S'git! You over-size excuse fer a lizard! I ain't fixin' to trust no gator further than I kin tail-toss one!"

There were those in the swamp who contended that Shovel Nose had more sense than Dad Peps, and possibly the gator's sudden retreat substantiated the theory. Shovel Nose didn't wait to contest the issue as Dad had. Off he went for the water under a shower of well-aimed rocks and cuss words, and he didn't consider himself properly safe until he was half-buried in the mud bottom of a stagnant pool.

* * * *

Instinct had a new bulletin for him: he'd just made another enemy.

Out in the palm bog Dad and Hughie didn't stop running until their gasping lungs refused to help them any further, and then Hughie plopped on the marshy earth like a dropped glass of water and began having himself a panting good time, but Dad stayed on his feet because he was so pure-out mad he didn't realize how winded he really was. Hughie didn't bother to start a conversation; he knew that just as soon as Dad found some wind he would hog the pulpit.

And he was right. First off Dad heaved his pulpy old felt hat *splat* against a cypress tree, and then he really cut loose.

"Well, *hit* myself!" he shouted. "Beat myself and turn myself inside an' out and *throw* myself away ifn I'm a-goan have it! Never in all my bornt days have I seed sech a crampy broom-swingin' mouth-shoutin' old witch as thet air widder woman! Broom-bust my haid, will she? Call me shoat-thief, does she? I'll show her shoat-snatchin'! I'll show—"

"Dad, Dad," Hughie wailed. "You ain't fixin' to try an' go at the widder's shoats again, air you? Because I tell you cold I ain't aimin' to git *my*self shotgunned in the seater."

But Hughie was talking to a brick wall, because next to trying to catch Shovel Nose and hide-sell him, Dad liked to catch someone else's shoat and skillet-fry it.

"Hughie," Dad said with fatherly patience, "will you kindly shet thet ear-bangin' mouth a yorn afore I go to wrop a cypress knee about hit? How you kin be so bat-blind an' be a son of mine I'll *never* know! Cain't you see when I got me a plan?"

"Yeah, but thet ol' widder got her a *shot*gun."

"Hesh yer biggity mouth," Dad admonished him. "Listen at yer ol' dad…we goan use us some *strat*-gee."

"What's thet?"

"Thet's what Stonewall Jackson used to whup the Yankees with. Now look a-here, Hughie. Thet widder woman thinks she gone cleared the field an' won her the day. She don't reckon on seein' you'n me fer a month a Sundays…and, boy, right thar is whar we goan fool her. Hek! Hek! 'Cause you'n me is goan at them shoats agin tonight when she least egg-spects us to. Now thet air's what I call *strat*-gee!"

"Well," Hughie muttered doubtfully. "Well…"

But Dad's mind was drifting off in cooking-pot fantasies. He rubbed his stomach and gazed dreamily at the distant cabbage palms.

"Mebbe I won't go to have me fried shoat right off the first night. Mebbe I'll have me sowbelly and wild salat. I'll boil me some mustard greens along with a chunk of thet air sowbelly an' then I'll git me my vinegar bottle and…"

* * * *

The night crept in on soft black cat feet, and an expectant silence hovered over the swamp like a glass ball tottering on the edge of a shelf. It shattered abruptly when a far-out hound cut across a timber wolf and loosed his night-running bay, and immediately a flock of night-feeding ducks took off, flicker-flacking their wings in the moonlight, and for minutes after everything was music.

Shovel Nose waited in the maiden cane, watching the lamplight in the Widow Harks' shanty, listening absently to the night.

Abruptly the light winked out and the shanty became a square block of blackness. The gator waddle-sloshed out of the tules and nosed himself into the water. Keeping carefully in the shadows, he drifted by the sandbank and then took a turn to the left.

Along the south edge of the widow's yard ran a short and shallow backwater that petered-out in a ditchlike ravine, all choked with elderberry and catclaw bush and tules. Shovel Nose tail-hitched into the setback, the tip of his snout and his knobby eyes protruding above the surface, his earflaps open and in tune with the night.

Everything was still again. A lone buzzard cut across the glazed face of the moon, but without sound. Shovel Nose eased his scut-plated body from the water and wedged himself into the thicket. He squirmed and shoved for thirty-some feet into the reeds and catclaw, and then scrabbled up the side of the ravine and flattened himself in the sawblade grass in the widow's backyard, pretending he was a worthless log.

He studied the moonlit yard, eying the shadows and henhouse and pigpen suspiciously. Nothing moved. His scooplike lower jaw, turning up at the rear, suggested that he was smiling over something. He raised on his unwieldy legs and lumbered five-six yards toward the pigpen and then dropped in a shadow pool and made like a log again.

It was while waiting and listening this second time that he suddenly heard the rustling sound of something coming cautiously through the palmetto fronds.

Easy, like two weasels sneak-prowling, Dad and Hughie slipped from the scrub and into the yard. Dad led the way on tippy-toes, coming straight for the pigpen and the shadow pool, where Shovel Nose was playing dead-log. Dad was carrying an old gunny sack to help tote his sowbelly dinner home.

They crept into the shadow with Shovel Nose and paused.

"I cain't hear me a sound outn them porkers," Dad whispered. "Do yer think thet widder woman went and tookt 'em into the house?"

"Mebbe they's all asleep in the hutch, Dad."

Dad grunted and said, "Goan scramble me up on this here ol' log an' see kin I look in thar and spot 'em."

Shovel Nose couldn't believe it when Dad suddenly hoisted himself on his scutted back. His instinct split into two tributaries—half rushing off in wild fright, and the other half quivering into burning anger. Dad, in the past, had pulled a lot of tricks to try to capture him, but he'd never gotten on his back before.

Shovel Nose began raising his ponderous upper jaw. "D-Dad—" Hughie stuttered. "I don't think—"

"Ain't nobody a-askin' you to," Dad whispered fiercely. "Shet up, and stop a-teeter-totterin' the log."

"B-but, Dad, I don't think you be standin' on no log."

"Well then I'd kindly like to know what in juckies I *be* stan— *WHAAA!*" Dad let out a bellow as Shovel Nose pivoted his come-to-life body from the center, his armored tail swishing one way and his yard-high open mouth swinging the other.

Dad's balance went out of whack with the gator's sudden momentum, and he spilled boots-over-beanie into the pigpen with a splash, while Shovel Nose—losing sight of him—snapped at Hughie, who was now standing all agape directly in front of him, and to Hughie it was like a great iron gate clanging shut, and he let out a cry that had the intonation of a latter-day rebel yell.

"Eeee-YOW!"

Hughie took off across the yard, high-stepping it for the bush with Shovel Nose hot on his shirttail, and Dad was all over mud and broken pigpen and knocked half witless, and the pigs were squealing and the hens were squawking, and then the widow's worthless old hound finally woke up and came out of his shed barking a storm, and the next thing Dad knew the rear door of the shanty kicked open and the Widow Harks was up there on her porch with a double-barreled 12-gage, and the only part of her yelling that Dad understood was when she shouted:

"I see you, Dad Peps! You no-account shoat-stealin' critter!"

And then Dad's legs were underway like two tumbleweeds coming down a road in a windstorm, and the 12-gage went *KA-BLOWIE! KA-BLOWIE!* and buckshot went whizzing into the tupelo and titi, and Dad was long gone for the deep swamp.

When Shovel Nose heard the gunblast he forgot about Hughie and veered sharply for the creek. To his unreasoning memory the explosive sound had only one meaning: Dad was after him. He high-balled for the water just as fast as his stumpy legs could haul his clumsy body. He didn't have any idea what had happened or why. He was running now on pure instinct; and instinct was getting him home to his den just as quickly as it knew how.

* * * *

The things that Dad did to his hat that night out in the swamp shouldn't be done to a rusty old tin can that nobody wants. He balled it in his fist, he ricocheted it off tree trunks, he kicked it and jumped on it, and when he couldn't find anything else to do with it—and it looked like it might still have some life left in it—he went at it with a stick and beat it to pie.

And then—after he'd finally run out of cuss names to tag onto Shovel Nose—he hunkered down in the hurrah bushes with the morose Hughie and started getting himself back in hand. First he shook the dirt and weed-bits from his old ruin of a hat and set it on his head, then he dug his fingers in his beard and gave it a good tugging (which helped his thinking), and then he grunted.

"Well," he said, "I've seen pure-out bad luck afore, but I never seen so much in one bucket."

"You got hit to come at. Dad," Hughie said. "You be licked."

"*Licked! Licked!* Be dogged if I be! I got my sights set on a shoat dinner an' thet's jest what I'm a-fixin' to eat!"

"Well, I ain't goan git myself gator-et er seater-shot fer hit," Hughie asserted.

But Dad had a sly look in his wicked old eyes.

"Hesh up thet gate-mouth a yorn. I got me a think a-comin' on."

Hughie looked interested. There wasn't anybody as crafty as Dad; and when Dad started kicking an idea around in his brain-box, the swamp had just best look out.

"What say, Dad?" he prompted.

"A *dee*-coy," Dad said. "Thet's what I'm a-fixin' on."

"What's thet, Dad?"

But Dad only chuckled and tugged away at his beard. *Hek! Hek!*

* * * *

One thing Dad and Shovel Nose had in common: when the idea of a shoat dinner entered their heads there was simply no way of getting it out. That was why Shovel Nose returned to the creek early the following morning as though magnetized. Not for a moment did he associate the shotgun with the widow; to his reaction-reasoning all guns belonged to Dad and Hughie. Rocks were the widow's weapons.

Downstream the bull gators were tearing up the morning silence with thunderous bellows of defiance and temper, and Shovel Nose, heeding the call as a part of a primordial ritual, bellowed back. No one seemed inclined to challenge him, so he hissed wetly and meandered on.

The day was long, sultry and drowsy. He drifted in and out through the hummocks and reeds, passing the widow's shanty at least a dozen times, caught some fish, had a nap or two, and a sharp little tiff with a young gator he caught nosing around the backwater.

And so the impatient day crawled slowly by like a wounded snake, and then the night shadows came.

The moon was gold-dollar proud and the light it shed turned to silver as it spread over the palms and cypress, over the pin-downs and titi and the creeks, water prairies and log litters. And the stillness came like a warning, and even the silly poor-joe birds and the deceitful limpkins were silent.

Shovel Nose surfaced like a prehistoric submarine and tested the quality of the night. Instinct satisfied, he wended his way quietly to the darkened backwater and slid into the reed and elderberry, and waited there patiently, as immobile as a dead sycamore in a choke-berry thicket, listening to the final *clucks-clucks* from the henhouse.

Moving with infinite caution he eased himself along the ravine until it petered out to sawblade grass. He plowed noiselessly through the weed and up and into the widow's backyard.

Immediately he went into his favorite act and became a useless old log in the shadows. His senses pulsated into the night and hurried back with dandy reports to his instinct. The field was clear. It was tasty shoat time! He went scrabbling across the yard, so low to the ground a coachwhip snake would have been squeezed to death under his white-tile belly.

He came within three yards of the pigpen and stopped again. One final check and then... A premonition of danger clanged his senses. Statue-still, his eyes popped with wonder, he listened, waited...waited....

Dad and Hughie slipped up the backwater in their battered old skiff and ran it aground in the maiden cane—completely blocking the exit to the creek, like a house parked in the middle of a country road. Dad had the gunny sack with him, but tonight the sack was just as busy and active as a kicked-over hornets' nest. Dad had a young crossback fox in the bag.

"I shore gosh wish you'd come to tell me what yer goan do with thet air crossback, Dad," Hughie whispered excitedly.

Dad looked just as sly and self-pleased as a raccoon in a cornfield when the hounds are away.

"This here's my *dee*-coy, boy. Goan set him loose in the henhouse."

"*Set him loose in the henhouse?* Lord a li'l hop-toadies, Dad, him 'n them hens will kick up a ruckus like a bear in a trap!"

"I know hit." Dad smirked. "I aim they should. This crossback is goan go at them hens and them hens is goan go all to squawkin' and thet widder is goan come bustin' outn the house jest a-lookin' fer trouble and she goan see this here crossback in her henhouse and she goan go at him like an eagle goes at a rattler, and cain't you guess what you'll me will be doin' while all thet fun's a-happenin'?"

Hughie's mouth was agape with amazement.

"Goan be gittin' us a fat old shoat fer dinner!" he whispered.

"*Kee*-rect! And thet, boy, is what yer old dad calls *dee*-coyin'."

"Well I never!" Hughie marveled.

"Git a-movin' thar," Dad ordered, "'stead a standin' about like a man with glue on his feet. Got us a sowbelly dinner a-comin' up!"

The two shoat snatchers scrambled through the thicket, following in Shovel Nose's trail, and then climbed out of the ravine and into the yard. Dad couldn't help *hek-hek*ing to himself when he eased up to the chicken yard and emptied the gunny sack over the fence.

The crossback fox landed on all fours, hunkered and bristling, and right now there was action. Dad and Hughie went hotfooting it for the ravine, leaving a bedlam of snarling and hen-squawking in their wake. The pigs started grunting and squealing, and the worthless old hound poked his snout out of his shed and went *Rrrrar-fff!*

Shovel Nose couldn't understand what was happening and what he couldn't understand he didn't go for at all. His tail began thrashing the weeds and his jaw started rising with apprehension. He heard the door of the shanty bang open and saw Widow Harks come out with her 12-gage.

"Who's thet after my hens?" she demanded.

Instinct gave Shovel Nose a healthy prod. It was time to ramble. He pivoted about in the darkness and started to get underway—and saw Dad and Hughie emerge from the ravine, coming right at him in a running crouch. His fright-reaction was involuntary and immediate. He swung his jaws open, sucked air into his great lungs and let her rip.

Gator thunder rumbled over the yard. The earth shook, the shanty windows rattled, the old hound balked in terror and took off for the scrub ky-ying, the crossback fox scooted under the henhouse, Dad skidded to a halt, and Hughie slammed into his back, and the Widow Harks swung around with the 12-gage, crying: "Land a Goshen! What's thet?"

Shovel Nose lumbered pell-mell for the ravine, and when Dad and Hughie saw him coming—running with his flat head parallel to the ground and his mouth open and showing them his remarkable rows of stoblike teeth—they forgot all about their shoat dinner.

"Feet—" Hughie cried, "show thet gator some heels!"

The three of them hit the ravine like a gone-crazy twister, choke-berry, elderberry, catclaw all a-smash, and the 12-gage going *KA-BLOWIE!* at the churning thicket, and Dad leaping a good yard ahead of Hughie, and shouting, "Git outn my way, you blame idjut! *I'm yer paw!*"

They came thrashing through the maiden cane and reached the skiff just four seconds before Shovel Nose. In they piled, both trying to get ahold of the stob pole at the same time and getting nowhere, and right at that moment Shovel Nose saw the skiff looming in front of him.

No room to go around it, no water space to go under, and being skiff shy he wasn't about to climb *into* it…so he snout-rammed it with everything he had.

The skiff scooted down the backwater, rearing high in the bows and shipping water over the stern, and Dad and Hughie tumbling all over bait can, fishing lines, gator-grabbing ropes, oars, stob pole and each other. Hughie came lurching to his feet, clutching the pole, and started shouting.

"Set on thet thwart, you worthless type a Dad, and git a-workin' them oars! I want outn here!"

But Dad couldn't seem to get his right foot free of the bait can.

"Set on the thwart!" he roared. "I cain't set me *nowhere!* I been pure-out buckshotted *in the seater!*"

Shovel Nose didn't know or care what happened after that. He submerged himself and scurried off to find a nice black morass to hide in. His instinct for shoat dinners was a thing of the past.

* * * *

In the warm glare of new morning Shovel Nose waddled onto the sandbank in a state of sulky dissatisfaction. He'd gone shopping for fish and couldn't find any, and then he'd chased a water turkey across the slough but it had flapped into the air too quickly. He was hungry and disgruntled. He hauled himself up on top of his favorite log and became a part of it.

He dozed with one eye half-cocked, and when he suddenly saw the Widow Harks standing at the top of the bank his instinct warned him of more trouble coming in the shape of rocks. But the Widow Harks just stood there looking down at him, holding something large and bulky in her hand.

"Hello there, you fat old riptile," she said. "You make some watchdog." And then she threw the bulky something down on the sand and walked off.

Shovel Nose didn't know how to react to the situation. He'd been ready to run until he saw her go away, and now he wasn't sure what he should do. He slid off the log and waddled over to the sandy object and gave it a good snoofing. It was a big meaty hambone.

The meal finished, Shovel Nose returned to his log and settled down for his nap. Instinct told him it was safe to sleep with both eyes closed.

CHAPTER 4

THE SHORE-FIRE TRAP

The morning was as bright and sparkly as a washed window when Dad and Hughie left their shanty and climbed aboard their old skiff. Dad made himself a comfortable seat in the bow on a great mound of ropy-looking material, and Hughie—as usual—was left to do all the work with the stob pole.

Dad was about to give Hughie the signal to shove off when he heard the *put-fut-fut-put* of a motorboat coming. Muttering darkly, he put his fingers in his fuzzly beard and gave it a tugging. The man in the approaching boat was the Fish and Wildlife warden of the swamp, and Dad would just as soon see a plague of locusts coming up the creek.

The warden cut his power and let the boat drift alongside the stationary skiff. He was a thoughtful never-in-a-hurry-to-speak type of man, and right now he just wanted to give the Pepses a contemplative (if not slightly suspicious) perusal.

Dad didn't appreciate people staring at him, especially game wardens, and he decided to give this one some strong lip service.

"Well," he said peevishly, "why you jest sittin' thar like a fool poor-joe bird? Ain't you never seen a gator grabber afore?"

Oh yes…the warden had seen plenty of gator grabbers in his time, but never one like Dad. Dad was the only gator grabber on record who couldn't out-run, out-maneuver or out-think a gator. Everyone in Okefenokee knew of the feud between Dad and Shovel Nose, and swamp folk were always retelling the tale about the time Dad had dropped a noose over Shovel Nose's snout and the gator had hauled him out of his skiff and into the water and through the log litter and maiden cane, leaving Dad feeling about as happy as an old work shirt that has just had a trip through a washing machine.

The warden gave a slow smile and said, "What's that you're sitting on, Dad? Some new contraption to catch gators with?"

"Thet's right," Dad said belligerently. "I'm a-settin' on a shore-fire gator-grabbin' net. And you don't need but one guess as to *which* gator I'm fixin' to catch in hit!"

"In a net?" the warden wondered. "Catch a gator in a net?"

"In a fishnet," Dad affirmed. "Ain't a gator a fish?"

"No," the warden said emphatically. "A gator's a reptile."

Dad mumbled and grumbled some and gave his straggly beard another mauling. "Well," he muttered disagreeably, "hit's purty near the same thing. And anyhow, fish er riptile, I'm a-goan' catch him this time, and I'm a-goan show him who he ben messin' with, and I'm a-goan whamp him 'n blamp him 'n twelve-gage him 'n..."

"Dad—Dad!" Hughie was whispering frantically from the stern.

Dad's mouth went into a wordless stall. In his fervor, he had forgotten just who he was talking to. Game wardens frown on gator-shooting.

"Dad Peps," the warden said sternly, "I don't want to catch you using a twelve-gage or any kind of gun on a gator, unless you have a permit. You know the law."

Dad became the picture of sly-eyed innocence. "Me?" he said incredulously. "*Me* shoot a gator? Why, Warden, I'd sooner go to shoot my boy Hughie thar than break the law by shootin' gators. Why, you kin ask anybody if I ain't the most law-upholdin' man they ever did see!"

"Oh?" the warden said. "Well, how did you come by that fish net?"

"Found it," Dad said promptly.

Hughie nodded his head energetically. That was so. Dad was the luckiest man he knew when it came to finding things. Of course, it was true that Dad's luck was of a nocturnal nature; he seldom found anything in the daylight, but when nightfall came... why, say, Dad could find loose pigs and frying hens and lost tools and Hughie didn't know whatall. Yessir! Dad was just pure-out lucky that way.

"*Hmm*," the warden said dubiously. "Well, as long as you try to catch Shovel Nose with a net and not with a gun, I don't give a hoot."

"*Try* to catch him?" Dad echoed. "Why, I blame shore am goan to catch him!"

The warden smiled. "In a fishnet? Bet you a dollar you don't."

That got to Dad. His ability was being doubted.

"Hughie, fetch me out thet dollar a yorn," he ordered.

"But, Dad," Hughie wailed, "thet's my yearly haircut dollar!"

"Laugh at yer yearly haircut," Dad advised him. "My gator-grabbin' reppy-tation is at stake. Fetch hit out."

Hughie, mumbling uncomplimentary observations about Dad's bullheadedness, rooted his dollar from his jeans, and Dad snapped it up like a trout taking a water bug and waved it before the game warden's eyes.

"Well," he said confidently, "I got my dollar and I'm a-puttin' hit in my pocket, where I 'spect yers will jine hit in a day er two."

"I'll be around to see," the warden said with a thin smile.

Dad snorted and gave Hughie an imperious order. "Shove off, you gawky-lookin' fool of a boy. Got me some gator-grabbin' to do!"

* * * *

If there was one thing Dad knew, it was Shovel Nose's habits and haunts. For weeks now he had made a secret study of the gator's activities and he knew exactly where Shovel Nose was living and at what times he could be found at home.

The trouble was, it was one of those far-out places in the swamp; so far out, in fact, that Hughie claimed the cottonmouths nested with the cooter birds because none of them knew any better.

But when Dad made up his mind to do a thing, he did it. And he didn't care what he had to go through to do it, either. He didn't care if Hughie had to stob the quarter-ton skiff up boggy little creeks and guzzles or if Hughie had to get chest-high in the sloughs and haul the balky skiff through thick beds of water lettuce or if Hughie fell overboard when the pole stuck in the mud or if Hughie nearly got himself gator-drowned or cottonmouth-bit or panther-clawed, because he, Dad, was going gator-grabbing come heck or high water, and that's all there was to it, by juckies.

But Hughie, after three hours of Dad's dogmatic determination, took a different view of the situation. His clothes were nothing but soggy rags and most of him seemed to be an adornment of pulpy water lilies and wispy strands of pickerelweed, his hands were blistered, his tongue hung over his lower lip, he had a bump on top of his head, and he was purely beat to a standstill. He collapsed like a wet ragbag, shaking his head.

"I'm pure-out bushed. I ain't stobbin' one push further."

"You don't got to," Dad informed him grandly. "'Cause we're here."

Dad stirred himself for the first time that morning. He stood up and looked around with a satisfied gleam in his eye and said, "Fetch the net, Hughie, and folly yer old dad."

Manhandling the fishnet through the swamp wasn't the easiest job in the world, Hughie discovered. The blame thing was about as bulky and cranky as a full-grown timber bear, and if anyone thought it was a joke to wrestle *that* through the palmettos and log litter and the sinkholes and the catclaw and pin-down bushes, then Hughie was ready to call that someone a shore-dab fool!

Dad, leading the way through the scrub, wag-wagged his hand behind him as a warning. "Easy—easy, boy," he whispered without looking around. "Shovel Nose's hide-hole is smack-bang ahead of us. We got to go at him slow." Then he looked back to see if Hughie was obeying.

He didn't see Hughie. He saw a great mound of fishnet in the path.

"Hughie?" Dad hissed. "Whar you got to, boy?" Then he spotted a familiar foot sticking from the bottom of the heap.

"Hughie? Is thet you in thar?" he wanted to know.

A muffled voice filtered up through the many strands of netting to ask, "Who else would it be?"

Dad looked disgusted. He ordered Hughie to stop trying to go to sleep in the middle of the job and to come out of there right now.

"Here's what we got to do. The mouth of thet hole is spang on the crick, so we goan lower the net underwater right in front a his door. Then we'll hide up on top a the bank with some lines runnin' to the far corners a the net. Then we'll jump up 'n down on Shovel Nose's roof, and when he comes tearin' out—*we snap the net overn him!*"

"But how do you know he be in thar, Dad?"

"*How do I know?*" Dad nearly came apart. "Hughie, what do you call thet thing on yer neck—a beehive with buzzings? Don't I know ever' move thet blame gator makes? Don't I have him pinned down to the very minute? Ain't hit now high noon? And don't he ever' day curl hisself up in his hide-hole from eleven to one fer a snooze? How do I know! C'mon now, 'stead a sittin' thar like a pumpkin in a field."

But the upshot was that Shovel Nose *wasn't* in his cave. And worse—after five hours of squatting in a nearby palmetto clump with the skeeters dogfighting around their ears and the little crawly bugs everywhere up their legs and down their necks and inside their shirts—it became apparent to them that Shovel Nose wasn't planning on returning.

"Mebbe he got hisself a new house, Dad," Hughie offered.

Well, it was more than Dad's patience could allow. He stood up, heaved his old hat *whamp!* against a tupelo trunk, and cried:

"Do you mean to sit thar an' tell me thet I went through all thet toil 'n troublesomeness fer *nuthin'*? You mean to say thet after fightin' thet blame ol' skiff 'n fishnet through ten miles a gafocky swamp I ain't even goan see Shovel Nose?"

Hughie nodded wearily. "And I ain't goan see no more a my yearly haircut dollar, neither," he complained. "Thet fool warden will be around soon to relieve you of hit."

It was too much for Dad to believe.

"Thet no-'count scut-sided bent-nosed gator has done it to me agin! He's cold cost me a hull day's toil an' he's gone an' cost me a hull dollar as well! Oh, I tell you! Ifn I could jest git my hands on thet blame riptile—*what I wouldn't do!* I'd twist him tailendto! I'd scut-shuck him like corn! I'd boot-stomp him 'n club-beat him 'n..."

Dad, in his excitement, had unwittingly fetched himself to the top of Shovel Nose's cave, and now he was leaping up and down on the roof, showing Hughie exactly the manner in which he was going to handle his old enemy when the day of reckoning came, and all at once the roof caved in, dropping Dad out of the world and into mucky darkness.

It was just as well that Dad was inside the cave, because the blue language he was using was enough to shock timber wolves. But by the time Hughie had hauled him out of the slush—Dad looking like a man who had absentmindedly taken a mud-bath with his clothes on—he had calmed down a mite.

"I jest don't know," Dad said in a moment of reflective melancholy. "Sometimes I git to wonderin' why I was bornt."

Which was exactly the way Hughie felt when he had to gather up the fat-type fishnet and lug it all the way back to the skiff by himself.

* * * *

It was nearly dark when Shovel Nose reached his cave. He had rambled far afield that day looking for a bountiful fishing hole, and what he had finally found had been a smooth-flowing guzzle that narrowed to a bottleneck between two tide hummocks. Dad's fishnet would have been excellent for the occasion, but Shovel Nose had to be content with what nature had endowed him: a big mouth. He had submerged his scutellated body in the bottleneck and every time a school of fish approached he would open his enormous jaws and transform himself into a natural fish weir. It had been a most satisfying day.

And now he was tired and ready for a nap...and that's when he discovered that his den had caved in.

Standing on his stumpy legs, his snout poking into the hole, he began thrashing the riverbank weeds with his angry tail. The huge mound of fresh dirt that covered his comfortable bed of slushy mud was one thing; he could clear that out in no time with his snout and paws. But the hole in the roof was something else again. *That* he could do nothing about.

He began grunting up a storm. His tail worked, his furious little eyes opened and closed, his claws dug into the peaty earth… lie let it rip. Gator thunder broke over the brooding swamp. The earth shook, tupelos trembled, cooter birds scooted, wildcats hissed and cowered in trees, a Hock of night-feeding ducks hit the sky, whamping the air with their wings. And then, as the thunder smoldered down to an irritated rumble, the swamp began shrieking its protest.

Shovel Nose tramped off under a steady barrage of cat-calls, bird cries, and snake hisses. He went house-hunting downriver.

* * * *

The morning found him floating quietly in the creek that fronted the Pepses' rattletrap old shanty. As soon as he saw Dad and Hughie leave the house with their fishing poles he went into his drifting-log act, submerging all of himself except his raised eye knobs. He watched them enter their skiff—Dad holding the fishing poles, Hughie the stob pole—and go on down Crick Crack and around the bend.

There was suddenly something very interesting about the old shanty in the swamp clearing. Namely, it was exuding a smell that attracted Shovel Nose's appetite, and anything that affected his appetite always attracted his curiosity.

With hardly a ripple to his wake he worked his laterally compressed tail, impelling himself to the shore. He then left the water by a cautious route: first into a tide bed, then a palmetto clump, finally into a stand of paint-root. He peered through the foliage at the clearing. Nothing moved. Time and swamp were stilled. Instinct tried to hold him back, but appetite prodded him into the open.

He waddled awkwardly across the clearing to the rickety porch steps. The door was open and the wonderful odor of cooking meat was unmistakable. He placed a horny paw on the bottom step and again he was bothered by a twinge of unseen danger, but once more appetite overrode instinct. He began slithering clumsily up the steps.

He stalled on the porch, snoofing and snorfing his snout through the doorway. The interior of the shanty wasn't such-a-much; a smoke-blackened limestone fireplace, a hacked-from-the-wilderness bed, table, dish hutch, benches. He couldn't detect anything harmful to a curious gator.

A fire was dancing in the grate under a big black pot that was hanging from a swivel hook. The pot was perking merry sounds—*Plop! Ploop!* and its odor drew him across the room as if he were magnetized.

He gave the black pot a shove with the tip of his snout. The pot swung away an inch or two and then whipped back and gave him a bang on the nose. He eyed it speculatively, then gave it a harder shove. Boiling water sloshed over his snout and he snorted furiously, backing hastily away. What one end of him couldn't whip, the other end could. He maneuvered himself into a fresh position and swung his heavy tail.

Bubbling water, Dad's sowbelly dinner, iron pot, all came clanging and splashing over his tail. It didn't really hurt him but it was frightening. He scurried to the door, fanning his tail behind, and looked outside. Satisfied that he still had the place to himself, he turned back and went after the steaming sowbelly.

It was the first hot meal he had ever eaten and he didn't mind it at all. Finished, he looked hopefully around the room with a gatorgrin. Maybe there was something else tasty to be found.

"Fergittin' the bait can!" Dad's crampy voice cried in the clearing. "Beat myself with old stob poles if I ever seed sech a fool type a boy! Hit cold whips me how you kin live with *me* so many years an' still be so all-fired witless. Didn't I go to lam you ever'thin' you know?"

"Well, lord a grasshoppers, Dad, how was I to know you went and put thet bait can in the cooler? I thought hit were in the skiff."

Thump-thump-thump on the porch steps. Shovel Nose swiveled himself about to face the doorway. Instinct gave him two cardinal rules to cover such a situation: if possible, run; if trapped, fight. He unhinged his jaws and started for the door.

Dad came stamping in with a mouthful of complaints.

"I teached him 'n cussed him 'n whapped him with sticks, and still he don't larn nuth—" Then he saw Shovel Nose coming at him, all teeth, and Dad jerked to a dead stop.

"*WHAA—!* Great hoppin' herons, how did—"

But it was no time for questions. Dad grabbed the door as he leaped back to the porch, looking as spry as a scarecrow in a windstorm.

The door slammed in its frame and Shovel Nose's teeth slammed on the door and he couldn't understand it because he didn't know about doors. Where had his escape passage gone? He blinked and grunted and then brought his tail around and started beating an angry tattoo on the shaky door.

Dad was still clutching the door latch outside, and he was bouncing and jerking and trying to gasp words through his excitement and not making it at all, and Hughie was trying to get him by the elbow and hold him down to earth.

"Heyday, Dad!" Hughie cried. "What you got in thar?"

"Wha…what…" Dad finally got his mouth going. "What do I *got?* I got me *Shovel Nose* in thar, *thet's what I got!* Quick now, Hughie—shutter the winders, fetch a deadlog agin the door, plug the chimney… Shake yer feet, boy! Move! Hop! Jump when I tell yer to!"

Hughie looked like a boy who was trying to meet himself coming and going. He was three places at once and doing five things at a time and all the while Dad was helping him by hopping up and down on the porch.

"*Hughie!* Hughie boy! Git the hammer 'n nails, you thinkless type a idjut! Hughie! Git the cotton-pickin' log! Hughie—!"

Hughie, run ragged, finally went plop in the yard and let his lungs pant about for some air. "Got…got her done, Dad," he gasped.

"*Great day in the mawnin'!*" Dad bellowed. "I done caught me Shovel Nose at last! I purely have gone an' done hit!"

Hughie perked up rapidly. "Thet's the talk, Dad. And by juckies, we've gone an' won us thet dollar too!"

But something was happening inside the shanty. Shovel Nose had finally realized that he was in an inescapable trap, and his surprise, fear and rage exploded in a gator roar that threatened to burst the board siding of the shanty. *BARRR-OOOM!*

Shakes started clattering off the roof, windowpanes shattered behind the shutters, pots and pans and tin plates rattled out of the hutch, one of the porch supports jerked loose and fell on Hughie's foot and the overhang sagged dangerously toward Dad's head, and Dad legged it down those steps like a man leaving a sinking ship.

"Here now!" he cried excitedly from the safety of the yard. "What's happenin' to my house? Hit looks like bombs is goin' off in hit!"

But Hughie was only capable of one thought at a time.

"Laugh at the house, Dad! *We got us ol' Shovel Nose!*"

Dad, however, had a slow-dawning look on his seamy face.

"Now wait a minute here," he said. "Somethin's gone wrong somewheres. We got him trapped in thar, *but our guns is in thar with him*. Now what I want a know is—*how we to git him out?*"

"Burn the house down!" Hughie cried.

Dad tore at his beard. "Burn the house down! Hughie, I swar when they went to passin' out brains you must a ben off fishin' er some—" His wicked little eyes sparked with sudden inspiration.

"*THE FISHNET!* Hughie, you thumb-handed fool, fetch thet fishnet! Hek! Hek! Now I got him, the four-leggit spade-snouted worthless…"

So, at Dad's bombastic direction. Hughie spread one end of the huge net on the porch in front of the door and then brought the bulk of it out from under the overhang and lugged it up onto the roof.

"Now!" Dad rubbed his hands. "I'll come up thar where you be and you come down here an' open the door. Then, when thet stupid riptile comes a-chargin' out, I'll drap the rest a the net overn him!"

But Hughie wasn't too crazy about the arrangement.

"Why cain't I stay up here and *you* open the door?" he wondered.

"Hughie," Dad said sternly, "is thet a way to talk? What if somethin' might go wrong? You know I cain't run near so spry as y'all."

"Well, I shore ort a be spry," Hughie grumbled. "I've had to cold out-run a heap a gators thet you've sicked on me."

But it didn't really matter how they arranged it, because Shovel Nose wasn't about to come outside and get himself netted. He didn't know a thing about fishnets but he knew plenty about Dad and Hughie; mainly that every time they saw him they shot at him, and now his instinct warned him that he was much safer inside the shanty than outside.

So, when Hughie removed the deadlog and gingerly opened the door, Shovel Nose was hiding under the bed and all he did was hiss at Hughie. He wouldn't budge, not even an inch of tail.

Then Dad lost his temper and jumped up and down on the roof to scare Shovel Nose out but the gator wouldn't scare and Dad's foot went through one of the rotten shakes and all he got for his trouble was a wrenched ankle. Then Dad had Hughie crawl under the house and start a small fire to smoke Shovel Nose out but the under-planking started to smolder and Hughie had to make four frantic trips to the creek with water buckets and they had to stop that nonsense. Then Dad had Hughie butcher one of their prize shoats and they placed it in the net in the doorway to tempt Shovel Nose out and still the blame gator wouldn't stir.

And finally Dad had a hopping fit right in the middle of the yard and got himself so mad he threw rocks at his own house and one of them smashed an oil lantern he kept on the porch.

It was enough to make a man cry. So Dad did. He cried terrible words until his voice cracked and fell Hat. After that he just thought 'em.

* * * *

Night brought the skeeters and all the little crawlies that no one in his right mind had any use for, and Dad and Hughie couldn't even have a fire to help combat them because all the matches were in the shanty with Shovel Nose and Hughie wasn't worth a bag of beans at rubbing two sticks together. So Dad sat on a stump and tugged his beard. He was beginning to wonder if he and Hughie had Shovel Nose trapped in the shanty or if Shovel Nose had them trapped in the clearing.

"The blame riptile's got our matches, our guns, our corncob pipes, he's had our sowbelly fer dinner, an' right now I bet a purty he's sprawlin' his fat self on ray bed!" Dad muttered unhappily.

"Well," Hughie offered helpfully, "we kin always starve him out."

"No, we cain't!" Dad fumed. "We ain't got thet much time. Tomorry mornin' thet warden is bound to come along and he's goan say, 'Well, I see you ain't caught Shovel Nose in thet fishnet, so where's my dollar?' Now why did I ever let you talk me into a fool bet like thet?"

"Let *me* talk *you* into hit?" Hughie cried.

"Oh, hesh yer biggity mouth an' go to sleep!" Dad ordered.

But how could a man get any sleep when he was busy all night slapping his ears and nose free of skeeters and chasing all through his clothes after the crawlies? And long about dawn a fat old honey bear wandered into the yard to see what was doing and when Dad called him mean names and threw rocks at him, he went off in a huff and knocked down Dad's woodpile, and there was another nice mess for Hughie to take care of.

"I want my mornin' coffee!" Dad cried childishly. "I ain't *about* to set out here an' drink slobby old slough water!"

"Mebbe Shovel Nose will let you have a cup when he's done with hit," Hughie said spitefully.

Dad glared at him. "Ifn I had me my carbine, you kin bet I'd go in thar an' kindly bullet-hole thet house-stealin' riptile." Abruptly he clamped his mouth shut and his mean little eyes went sly.

"Hughie—I got me an idee a-steamin' in my brain-box. Hek! Hek!"

Hughie shuddered. He knew Dad's ideas.

"You know how gun shy thet air Shovel Nose be," Dad prompted. "When he hears him a gun he's long gone fer the far-out titi."

"Yeah, Dad, but he's got all our guns," Hughie reminded him.

Dad grabbed up a handy stick and tried to whap the nimble Hughie with it.

"You stone-haided excuse fer a boy! *I* know he's got the guns. What I'm fixin' on is makin' him *think* we got a gun out here; makin' him think we're a-comin' at him with a carbine. Now shet yer gate-swingin' mouth an' listen at yer dad. Here's what we uns do...."

* * * *

Minutes later Operation Fool-the-Gator was in effect. Dad was up on the porch roof with the great bundle of netting in his spindly arms and Hughie was standing at the rear of the shanty with a long one-by-six board in his hands.

"Let her crack, boy!" Dad called.

Hughie stepped back and swung the board flat against the rear wall.

PAA-LAM! Shovel Nose, hiding under Dad's bed, started up in a panic. He knew he had just heard a gun and his instinct had only one thing to say: *Get* going. He charged for the open door and the underside of the bed hooked on his scutellated back and bed went with gator, and table, benches and hutch went with bed, and when Shovel Nose hit the doorway everything else hit the door frame and was splintered to matchwood.

The appalling crash only served to frighten the poor gator into greater speed. He had no idea what the spider-webby thing was that hung down over the porch, but it didn't look like much. He charged into it snout-first and went blundering down the steps.

Dad, observing the action from above, yelled, "Got yer now!" and dropped the rest of the net. Unfortunately, Dad had not observed that his left foot was entangled in one corner of the net and all at once he looked like a man who had just stepped into a well.

The three of them came together at the foot of the stairs—gator, net and Dad. Gator then tried to go one way, Dad another, and the net was going everywhere. It was awful, just awful.

Shovel Nose couldn't understand what was up—or down. He could see through the net, he could even run in it somewhat, but he couldn't get away from the crazy thing. And it felt like he was dragging a petrified log behind him.

It was Dad—wildly tangled in the net.

"Hu-Hu-*Hugh-EEE!* Git the—the—" Dad's words were cut short as Shovel Nose took off through the demolished woodpile, dragging the helpless Dad—*bump—bumpity-bumpbumpbump*—after him.

"Hugh-*EEE!* Git the blame car-car-*carbine!* Hep yer old dad, boy!"

Hughie came around the end of the shanty and saw Dad being bounced first one way then another, here, there, all over the gafocky yard. Dad's head ringing sounds wherever Shovel Nose hauled him—*BONK!* off a log. *DONK!* off the corner of the henhouse. *WHONK!* on the pigpen railing. And suddenly a new sound entered the chaos… *Put-fut-fut-put!*

"I cain't shoot him!" Hughie cried. "Here comes thet fool warden!"

Rut it was too late to matter. Shovel Nose had finally straightened his course and off he went for the river—through the paintroots, the palmettos, the tule bed, and lumbered spang into the water, Dad merrily bouncing right along.

Now Shovel Nose was at home. His panic diminished as he sank to the mucky bottom and went to work on the pesky netting with his teeth. In a moment he'd torn a large exit hole for his body and he took off for the distant shadows, letting Dad have the entire net to himself.

Dad looked like a man who had been fired from a cannon into a tub of water when the warden and Hughie hauled the net up and landed him on the beach. The warden shook his head and said:

"Well, lie's as ornery and bullheaded as a gator, but the fact remains he isn't one. And the bet was that he'd catch Shovel Nose in the net. Not himself. So I want my dollar."

All Dad could say was *Blup* and *Blaugh* and other wet words like that. Hughie sighed and went to work pulling the soggy Dad from the net.

"You know," he said, "sometimes I think thet ol' Shovel Nose is more human than gator. Yestiddy Dad went an' ruint Shovel Nose's hide-hole, and now looky how Shovel Nose went an' got back at him."

CHAPTER 5

THE WONDERFUL FOUNTAIN OF YOUTH

Shovel Nose slithered his unwieldy bulk through the palmettos and paint-root and catclaw thickets and down to the muddy silt-bank where thirty-some gators were basking their scutellated bodies in the sun. He waddled onto the sloping bank and stood on his stumpy bow-legs, cocking his head first right, then left, and gave a friendly snorfle to let the napping gators know that he had arrived.

None of them seemed to care. They grunted and snorted and thrashed their tails a bit and continued to doze. Shovel Nose, tramping and sliding good-naturedly over them, prowled about looking for a nice warm muddy spot for his own siesta.

Unwittingly he tromped on the wrong gator—the wrong gator's flat snout, to be exact.

Instantly the irate gator began grunting-up, making a noise like a donkey engine building up enough pressure to explode. Then, abruptly and completely, he did. Gator thunder boomed and rolled and caromed off the slough's surface. The siltbank vibrated, the porous earth quaked, palmetto fronds trembled. Shovel Nose turned with surprise and beheld his second worse enemy (Dad was his first worse), the great bull gator.

The great gator unhinged his ponderous jaws, hissed, and made a beeline rush at Shovel Nose. His open mouth looked as big and unfriendly as a manmade bear trap studded with sharpened stakes.

It was really no fight at all, because Shovel Nose had learned the wisdom of retreat at an early age. He and the great gator had tangled before, to Shovel Nose's discomfort. He took off for the slough in a panic of hurry, coming off the bank and into the water like a mill log down a chute. The great gator stood defiantly in the shallows and roared—roared—roared after him.

Shovel Nose tail-hitched himself angrily upstream. He was mad clear through; ready to fight anything, almost—except the great gator. And that was why it turned out to be a bad day for old Doc Weems.

* * * *

"Doctor" O. (for Oswald) L. Weems was, among many many other things, a self-made self-appointed medicine man. He traveled the back hills and swamplands peddling his utterly worthless "Dr. O. L. Weems Marvelous Metamorphic Magical Medicine" to the hillbillies and swampbillies for a dollar per pint bottle or a dollar six-bits for two.

Now it seems that Doc's supply of Marvelous Metamorphic had run dry while he was making his rounds in the swamp and so he had found himself a little spring that emptied into Crick Crack Creek and had proceeded to set up his laboratory.

His arrangements were simplicity itself. He constructed a firebox of stones directly above the spring, got a fire going, placed his huge old copper kettle over it and set his rack of empty bottles alongside. Then came the pouring in and stirring and stewing of the wonderful ingredients of the Marvelous Metamorphic.

First, a generous portion of nice fresh spring water, along with a little swamp silt to give the Marvelous Metamorphic body. Then a gallon of witch hazel to give the Marvelous Metamorphic kick. Then some herbs and roots and grubs right out of the bog nearby (and maybe even a lizard or somesuch because Doc's eyes weren't what they used to be since he misplaced his specs) to give the Marvelous Metamorphic tone. And finally the contents of a bottle of vanilla extract to give the one and only "medicine" flavor.

The gosh-awful brew now perking and steaming and bubbling merrily away, Doc set aside his slimy stirring-stick and proceeded to brush up on his selling spiel.

"Brothers," he announced to the cabbage palms and palmettos, "do you suffer from itching of the nose, itching of the scalp and even itching of the feet?" (It had been Doc's discovery that swamp folk—not prone to taking baths—itched more or less all over and all the time.) "Do you wake up at night and find you can't sleep?

Do you have spooky dreams when you do sleep? And when you wake in the morning do you find unhealthy grit in your eyes and does your tongue and mouth feel dry like you'd been chewing sand in your sleep and do you have a dull buzzing in your head before you take your morning coffee? And, brothers—worst of all—do you wake up and find red bumps all over your body which you *think* are skeeter bites?

"Do you ever have horrible dreams where you're stuck in quicksand and a wounded bear is coming at you? Or that you're falling into a palm bog full of gators? Or that you're lost in a pin-down thicket full of cottonmouths?" (It had also been Doc's discovery that this kind of nightmaring was very common and normal among people who lived in the swamp.) "Well, brothers, if you suffer from any or all of these dire, dire complaints, then you've got delirium-trembulums, which is a regrettable condition of the liver and which—"

And just at that point Doc thought that *he* was having an attack of the delirium-trembulums because right then and there and about as gracefully as a bulldozer leveling a thicket, Shovel Nose came crashing through the scrub and into the little clearing around the spring.

Shovel Nose had been attracted by the fragrant odor of the stewing Marvelous Metamorphic and he'd come waddle-legging for all he was worth, instinctively knowing that something good to eat was on hand.

But now he was momentarily nonplused because the only edible thing he could see in the clearing was Doc Weems. And that was just the way old Doc saw it too.

Doc had lived a long and fruitful life simply by trusting in one golden maxim: *If you can't beat 'em—leave 'em.* And he did and right now, his legs spinning like wheels on a downhill grade, and so fast they were still spinning when he came off the bank and into the air over the creek. But it didn't matter because his trusty rowboat was waiting right below and Doc came down like he meant to go right on through the bottom, and didn't wait to fool with his cranky old outboard motor but snatched up the oars and started rowing like he was being paid for it, before he remembered that the bow was aimed at the shore and that all he was doing was forcing the boat further onto the bank instead of away from it, and he yelled at himself, "What am I *doing*!" And then he started backwatering and he was still doing it as he disappeared around the bend in the creek.

Shovel Nose watched him go and sent a wet hiss after him. Doc's frantic retreat made him feel like a new gator. It restored his confidence in his reptilian prowess. It also restored his curiosity, which was as persistent as a summer fire in cornstalks. He ambled back to the spring to inspect the aromatic kettle.

He'd bumped snouts with fire before and he wasn't about to be burned twice. So he hitched his scutted body around and let the firebox have a good one with the flat of his lateral-driving tail. Stones flew apart, kettle overturned, the rack of empty bottles spun glassily in the air and everything disappeared into the quietly bubbling little spring.

Shovel Nose snorfed and grunted complainingly. Gone—all gone. He waddled into the spring, lowered the transparent lids over his eyes and submerged his snout and head. The well of the spring was barely larger than the top of a rain-barrel but it was deep, too deep to see to the bottom. He raised his head and opened his mouth to grumble and took in a quart or two of water.

Suddenly the fire that he thought he had destroyed was in his stomach. He snorted furiously and lumbered out of the spring. Then he stopped dead and cocked his flat head far to the right and stared vacantly at the palmettos. The naturally up-curving line of his jaw gave him a foolishly grinning aspect.

He decided to move. But something seemed wrong. As a rule he walked like any four-legged beast: right fore and left hind moving together, followed by left fore and right hind. It was no longer so. His right legs moved at the same time, tipping him leftward, then they crashed down and the left ones went up as his long body rolled to the right.

And that was the way he reentered the palmetto thicket, like a mastless ship on a tossing sea.

* * * *

Old Doc Weems had been put out of business before (usually by cranky sheriffs and irate mobs; never by gators) and he had developed a maxim to cover any such unpleasant proceedings: *If you have to abandon your line of business—sell your stock for whatever you can get.*

So Doc gave the situation some deep thought and decided to sell his interest in the hidden spring. He drew up a collection of maps, all duplicates, and that's practically all there was to it.

Humming a cheerful little tune, he got his outboard chug-chugging and started downstream. Dr. O. L. Weems was in business again, and his first suck—uh customers were to be Dad and Hughie Peps.

Doc stepped ashore before the Pepses' shanty and nodded genially to Dad and Hughie, pretending he wasn't even aware of the shotgun in Dad's hand or the long knobby stick in Hughie's, and said:

"Mawning, brothers, mawning! I'm Dr. O. L. Weems, Phd. Dip. and Pap. of archaeology, artifacts and aromatic arrobias. I have just made the discovery not only of *my* lifetime but of the world's dating back to the year 1502 and, brothers, the tragedy of it all is that under absolutely no circumstances physical, mental, organic or mineral can I put it to any personal use and so must sell the information to this miraculous world-shaking discovery to the first humans—" He caught himself a moment, glancing at Dad's beardy squinty unwashed face and at Hughie's gape-jawed blank-eyed countenance, and then continued:

"—uh to the first *people* I meet, and you, sirs, are them!"

Dad blinked and eased his eyes to Hughie to whisper, "Think I ort a kindly blow a hole in the pore fella an' put him outn his misery?"

But Hughie was fascinated by the machine-gun-like rapidity of Doc's words and he said, "Naw, naw. Dad. Let's hear about thet air world-shakin' discovery first."

"Thank you, son, thank you," Doc said hurriedly. "You've made a wise decision, and more than that—the decision that will turn all your wants, needs, desires, dreams, to gold, pure solid shining gold! Gentlemen—you behold before you a man who has dedicated the last thirty years of his life to the secret of this swamp and who today, not an hour past, fulfilled, accomplished, consummated that notable quest! Brothers, I have found Ponce de Leon's legendary Fountain of Youth!"

"Go on!" Dad gasped. "You ain't neither."

"I have though, brother, I have. Now you two—uh learned men know as well as I that four-hundred-fifty-something years ago Ponce de Leon knocked himself silly to find this fountain of natural magical properties in Florida and that ever since men from all over the world have—"

"But this here ain't Floridy," Dad offered. "Hit's Okefenokee."

Doc gave Dad a basilisk stare. "Brother, you know very well that Okefenokee covers most of Georgia as well as a goodly portion of the State of Florida, and if you can't point out to me a state borderline, then how can you say we *ain't* standing in Florida right here an' now?"

Dad had to admit Doc had something there; the truth being that Dad never had bothered to find out exactly what state he was living in.

"You made to mention a tray-jity," Hughie prompted.

"I did, young man, I did. A tragedy that has no equal in the annals of mankind. Thirty years I searched for the lost Fountain of Youth and on the very moment of my discovery I suffered a trauma. In short, I was attacked by an alligator."

Dad looked baffled. "You call a brush with a gator a—a whatsit?"

"A trauma," Doc affirmed. "A violent incident which leaves a psychological quirk in the brain. Like you'd stepped out a door and some fool went to drop a load of shakes on your head and ever after that your trauma wouldn't allow you to go through doors like normal folk but makes you climb in and out of houses through the windows. In other words, I must leave the swamp forever and the sooner the better, before I see another gator and go stark mouth-foaming mad."

Dad's sly little eyes grew bright with speculation.

"But you plan on *dee-sposing* of this air Poncy the Lion fountain afore you do, eh?" he urged.

Doc looked as though he were ready to tear his hair in despair.

"I must, brother, I must. Though it means the ruin of me. I have here a map I've made to the exact location of the fabulous fountain and, even though this map is worth thousands, hundreds of thousands, I—" He paused to give the Pepses and their shanty a quick mental appraisal. "I am forced to part with it for the absurd price of ten dollars. Cash."

Dad looked as if he had been hit over the head with a two-by-four.

"*Ten dollars!* Did you say *ten* dollars?"

"You heard me, brother. *One* dollar I said, take it or leave it."

So Dad took it…though Doc Weems had another way of putting it.

Hughie stobbed the skiff up Crick Crack Creek while Dad sat in the stern and twiddled his thumbs impatiently.

"Ain't they no way you kin move thet pole an' this here skiff faster along, Hughie?" Dad fussed. "I'd kindly like to git myself to my fountain sometime today!"

"Well, I don't reckon the idee to spell me on this pole ever snuck into thet hollow you tote around a-tween yer ears," Hughie complained. "I'm purely tired a stobbin' this blame ol' skiff!"

But Dad was in an affable mood. All he said was, "Soon's I sat-you-rate myself in all them magical properties of my fountain an' git my youth back, I'm goan give you sech a whoppin' you'll larn never to sass yer young dad agin!" Then he cackled and slapped his bony thigh.

"Jest think on hit, Hughie. Thar I'll be jest as spry an' sassy-fied as a twenty-year-old and I'll be able to run ol' Shovel Nose to earth ifn hit takes me fifty years!"

Hughie wasn't foolish enough to say it out loud, but he had it in the back of his mind that the Fountain of Youth would have to be a Fountain of Brains if it was going to help Dad catch Shovel Nose.

"Looky thar!" Dad suddenly whooped. "Ain't thet a guzzle a water I see a-sloppin' down thet bank? Bet yer pea-pickin' brain hit be! Lemme study my map here. Heyday, Hughie! Thar's the two-haided cabbage palm a-standin' back among the cypress jest like Doc Weems wrote down! Git thet air pole a-stobbin', boy! I kin hear Poncy the Lion's fountain jest a-gurglin' an' a-burplin' right now!"

Hughie ran the square bow of the skiff into the shelving bank and Dad nearly trampled him right into the floorboards getting by.

"Lemme at hit! Lemme at them magical youth-type properties! Fetch along my drinkin' cup, Hughie!"

Dad's spindly old legs carried him through the laurel thicket and into the clearing and up to the quietly bubbling little spring. He let out a whoop and dropped to his knees—nearly cracking both kneecaps.

"Hughie! Stop dawdlin' like a man in lead shoes an' git yer cabbage-haided self in here. *Gimme my cup!*"

Hughie gave Dad his tin drinking cup and hunkered down to peer suspiciously at the spring. "Looks kind a darksome," he muttered.

"Loooshkinshah—" Dad was already swilling down the wonderful liquid and he tried to talk through water, cup and all. Then he spat and spluttered and started all over. "Looks kind a darksome?" he cried. "Well, you don't 'spect a fountain full a magical properties to look like any ol' spring, do you? You beanbagbrained boy!"

But Hughie remained dubious. He scooped up a handful of the darkly gleaming liquid and gave it a sample taste.

"*BLAA-GAAH!*"

Dad reared back in shock. "Look out thar! Yer showerin' all over me! Have you gone out a yer club-haided mind?"

"*GLAAH-GLAAH!*" Hughie said. Then he said, "Lord a li'l jaybirds, Dad! Did you *taste* hit? Tastes like last year's stump water!"

"*Did I taste hit?*" Dad shouted. "Well, what's hit look like I'm a-doin? Washin' my feet in hit? 'Course hit tastes somewhat strongsome. Thet's them magical properties. Now go easy on hit. Don't drink too much. Don't want you shrinkin' down to baby size on me! Hek! Hek!" he laughed foolishly.

"Looky, Dad. Thar be some bottles down in the water thar."

Dad rolled his eyes like a couple of marbles on a tilted surface and said, "Thasso. What they be?" He stepped into the spring to investigate. Then, as long as he was partway in, he decided to go whole hog and speed up the youth-restoring process. He sat down in the water and chuckled.

"Hughie, boy! I simply feel the years drainin' offn me! How air I a-lookin'? Tell me thet!"

"Like a silly old man sittin' in a spring," Hughie told him.

"Hit's a blame lie! Bet I don't look a day over forty already. Thirty even. Wish I had me a mirror."

"Don't splash none in yer face, Dad," Hughie warned, grinning, "less yer whiskers fall off an' y'all have to go to wearin' a napkin to catch yer tobaccer juice!"

"Hughie, when I kindly step outn this spring, an' me only twenty, *you'd* best look out, is what!" Then Dad forgot about Hughie and picked up one of the bottles. "How'd these git here?" he wondered.

"Bet a purty diet ol' Doc was fixin' to bottle this water an' sell hit to folks, when the gator come at him," Hughie suggested.

"*Bottle this water!*" Dad cried, standing up in the spring with a bottle in each hand. "*Sell hit to folks!* Thet's the best blame idee I ever had me! Hughie, I'll be the richest daddy in Okefenokee! I'll sell my Poncy the Lion water up one crick an' down another! I'll—"

"Hi, Dad!" Hughie cried. "Yander come yer first customers!"

It was true. A small gang of swampmen were coming upcreek in their skiffs. There were seven or eight of them and altogether they were making almost as much noise as Dad. Seemed to be having an argument about something.

But Dad didn't care about their squabblings. He was all business.

"Hughie! Git in thet spring an' fetch up the rest a them bottles! I got to find me a lightwood stick an' cut some plugs to cap 'em with. I'm cold goan start makin' my first fortune right here 'n now!"

* * * *

Shovel Nose descended on the sleeping gator herd like an atomic war. Roaring, tail-swinging, jaws slamming like steel traps, he plowed a scut-flying path through them and launched himself at the great gator.

Doc Weems' Marvelous Metamorphic had transformed Shovel Nose into the king of gators—at least he felt like the king of gators. He was ready to take on anything within reason—from alligator to gunboat.

He lambasted the great gator up one end of the bank and down the other. He rolled the scutellated monster through paint-root and titi bushes and slammed him into maiden cane and log litter, and so upset three honey bears working a bee tree that they took off with their big round rump-ends swaying over their hairy pantaloon legs and lumbered smack into the agitated gator herd, spooking the reptiles completely.

Shovel Nose's fury convinced the great gator's instinct that his scoop-snouted enemy had gone mad. It also convinced him that it was time to be long gone. Trouble was, every time the great gator tried to make a break for the water Shovel Nose would cut him off and this flatly increased his panic. He took off inland in a hysteria of hurry, intent on finding another exit to the slough. The entire herd of thirty-some witlessly excited gators went lumbering after him.

Shovel Nose waddled along in their disorderly wake, bellowing victory. But not for long. A brand-new sensation was occurring within his armor-plated body. His stomach felt like a hollow log housing a rowdy family of raccoons. His head felt like a cypress knee being pounded by gator tails. *Thud-thud-thud.* He started slowing down. He felt sick. He felt like the oldest, most misused gator in Okefenokee.

He went home.

* * * *

Dad's customers came plowing through the laurels like wild Indians on a raid. There was Tote Beck in and his brother Mote, and Lon Camp dragging his old granddaddy along, and then there were the four Sempkins boys. All eight yelling up a storm.

"Well, hit blame shore is mine!"

"'Tain't! 'Tain't! Hit's a dirty lie!"

"Well, by grabbit, I got me the one 'n only map to prove hit!"

"You got the one'n only *lyin'est* mouth I ever heered an' thet's all you do got! I got the *true* map! Ol' Doc sold hit to me hisself!"

And old Granddaddy Camp, near to being run over in the rush, taking vicious cuts at their legs with his hickory cane, his cackly voice crying, "Now you fillers! You fillers listen at me now! I got me first dibs 'count a I be the oldest, somewhat! An' thet's a pure-out fact! Lon, you hear me, you worthless hollow-haided gran'son?"

Then Lon and the Beekin boys and the four Sempkinses all burst into the clearing and slammed to a startled halt. Dad was standing before them just as mean-eyed and cranky-mouthed and businesslike as he knew how to look. He was holding a bottle of spring water.

"Now, gents," he said authoritatively, "ifn you'll jest form yerselves in a tidy-type line, I'll start sellin' y'all my Poncy the Lion magical-propertied water. Because ifn er not you know hit—this here Fountain a Youth *belongs to me*. 'Count a *I* got here fustest!"

Well, he might just as well have thrown a scared skunk among them, the way they carried on. Tote said, "Hit tis, eh? Well, I'm fixin' to fetch my ten-gage an' blow you clean *offn* yer fustest!" And Sed Sempkins said, "An' I'm aimin' to find me a cypress branch an' whop yer skinny haidbone a-tween yer spindly shoulders, is what!"

But Lon Camp was gifted with a more legal turn of mind than the others and he said, "Now holt on a mite. Ifn Dad an' Hughie really have gone an' claim-staked this here fountain, then I reckon they got a lawsome right to her. But I'll say this: ain't no man goan sell me a pig-in-a-poke bottle 'lessn I know first hit *really* is Poncy the Lion water an' not jest any ol' bracky spring water."

And right about then old Granddaddy Camp came a-stumbling and a-lurching into the clearing, his hickory cane going one way and him going the other and the ground coming up to meet him, and he looked like a ninety-year-old man having a heart attack—

which wasn't at all true, because Granddaddy Camp was only eighty-seven and he was having a windpipe attack.

"Fi-fi-fillers!" he gasped. "Fetch me thet thar magical property water. I'm a-sinkin' fast!"

And he was, too. He sank right into the ground like a collection of old bones and whiskers in a patchwork bag.

"So!" Dad cried. "Y'all doubt the aw-than-tisity of my Poncy the Lion water, do you? Well, kindly step aside an' let Dr. Peps at the pore ailin' patient! Here, Granddaddy, jest you wrap yer toothless ol' mouth about the end a this here bottle. We'll soon see!"

They soon did. Granddaddy Camp belted home a healthy swig and right now his squinty old eyes popped open and out like a couple of golf balls and his hair stood on end and he opened his mouth and cut loose with a rebel yell.

"YEEE-YOOO-WO-WO-WOOO!"

Then he leaped to his feet and took a cut or two at the Sempkins boys' knees with his cane and let Dad have a dandy one in his belly-button with the end of the cane, like a playful fencer, and finally threw the cane away and started doing a buck-'n-wing in the clearing.

Dad rubbed his tender stomach first, then rubbed his hands together enthusiastically.

"Did I tell yer!" he crowed. "Did I *tell* yer! My Poncy the Lion water is pure-out magic! Hughie! Hughie boy, you got them bottles filled? All righty, gents, Dad Peps an' his Fountain a Youth is open fer business! Step up one'n all!"

"I don't feel a day over seventy!" old Granddaddy Camp whooped from the edge of the clearing. "Not a blame day over! I'm so young an' frisky I kin even hear thunder comin' from a hundred miles away!"

Dad's customers raised their brows and looked at each other and then looked at the glassy clear blue sky overhead. They could hear it too, coming closer and louder all the time.

"What is thet fool noise?" Dad wondered peevishly.

"Hit's a *hurry*-cane!" Hughie gasped.

"Hughie, if you ain't the most fool-haided son I ever did have me. How kin it be a hurry-cane when the sky's as clear as—as—"

But Hughie was right: it was a hurricane of stampeding gators—thirty-some of them—and they came smashing through the scrub and into the clearing just like they owned the place and didn't care a hoot whether Dad was trying to conduct his Poncy the Lion bottled-water business there or not. They were heading for the creek.

And they weren't the only ones.

Dad's customers took off like a crew of dogs with tin cans tied to their tails, and Hughie thought maybe there really was something to that spring water after all, because old Granddaddy Camp and Dad were just about as spry and agile as two ten-year-olds on the takeoff, and when it came to speed they made Hughie and Lon and die Beekins and the Sempkins boys look like they were stuck in quicksand.

Through the thicket and pell-mell down the bank and into the skiffs came the ten men and the thirty-some gators, all ankles-over-appetites in the stob poles and oars and fishing lines and bait cans, and Dad—somehow unwittingly—ending up sitting backwards on top of the scooting great bull gator's flat head and shouting at Hughie to "stob the blame pole faster!" and then seeing Hughie pull up alongside him in the skiff and having to make a hurried and mighty frantic transfer from one craft to the other, and nearly leaving the seat of his pants in the great gator's mouth in doing it.

After the gators had all submerged and disappeared, the Beekins and Camps and Sempkinses rearranged themselves in their skiffs and prepared to pole on downstream. Mote Beekins called to Dad.

"Might as well face hit, Dad. Yer long gone out a business. Doc Weems went an' sold you a map to a patch a gator ground. And anybody dumb enough to fool around on gator ground might jest as well throw hisself in a crick with a weight tied to his foot! See y'all later."

Well, Dad had some words to say about it to Hughie: cuss words mostly, all blue and mean and covered with the swamp water he'd swallowed when he came head-over-heels off the bank.

"Gators! Always hit's gators! No matter what I set out to do fer myself, some pesky gator will come slish-sloppin' along and bust hit all to gafocky on me! I tell you, Hughie, ifn I was to be standin' in the middle of a desert a-sellin' ice cream to the Ay-rabs, some fool gator would pop out a the sand an' chase me away an' eat all my ice cream as well. Yes, an' I'll bet anythin' you own thet his name would be *Shovel Nose*, too! I *tell* yer!"

"Now, now, Dad," Hughie temporized. "I reckon Shovel Nose does give you more grief than any other critter in this ol' swamp, but you shore cain't blame what happened today on *him*. Shovel Nose don't fool with no herd. He's a loner is what. Nossir. This is *one* time he didn't go an' git the best a you."

"Well, I don't know," Dad grumbled. "I 'spect yer right. But I jest got me a sneaky eeney-beeny feelin' thet *some*how, *some*way thet shovel-snouted riptile was behind... But, naw, I don't see how he *could* be. Well, you best git to stobbin' fer home, Hughie. Reckon I'll jest rest me a spell here. You know, hit's a funny thing but I don't feel so chipper all a sudden. My belly 'n haidbone feel like I et somethin' thet disagreed with me. Wonder now what hit could a been?"

CHAPTER 6

THE INCREDIBLE ISLANT

Shovel Nose had an advantage over Dad and Hughie: he didn't believe in ghosts. They didn't mean any more to him than a dead toad. But Dad and Hughie were swamp folk and superstition was a part of their ancestral heritage. It was as inherent in them as breathing or eating or trying their blame best to catch a gator. And anything that smacked of the supernatural-well, they simply took to it the way a field dog takes to a lame fox.

So that's why the haunted house on Beebie's Island didn't mean as much to the gator as it did to the gator grabbers.

Now Moaning Lake was a vast water prairie and it was clear to heck and gone somewhere at the back of beyond, which is quite a ways for a man or a gator to go—especially if the only thing he's going to find when he finally gets there is a lonely island and a beat-up old house in a stand of swamp oaks. But Shovel Nose had a reason.

You could just see the top of the house's tower from the water prairie. But that didn't mean you were getting close. First there was a tall bed of maiden cane, which wouldn't allow ingress to any skiff (and not much to any gator, either), and then a gosh-awful mess of cypress knees and log litter, and finally a dense thicket of hurrah and pin-down bushes with a few titi thrown in for good measure.

But none of this daunted Shovel Nose. He'd been to the island before and he had his own private crawl-through. He wobbled and scurried and scrabbled into the thicket and in no time at all he had his stumpy legs planted on the honest high earth of the island.

Being an incongruous mixture of caution and curiosity, the first thing he did was throw himself on the ground and make like a scabby old log that no one had any use for. His little obsidian eyes studied the deserted house.

The house was so old and beat it looked as if it might have been standing and waiting when Columbus missed America. It was one of those gaunt, weather-warped gingerbread affairs with shutter-blinded windows and half the shingles missing from the roof. There was a gallery running around the ground floor, and upstairs there was a gabled room on each of the four corners with the lookout tower in the center.

It looked like those houses you see in the horror movies, or in nightmares, with bats fluttering out of the belfry and the shutters banging in the wind, and you *know* that a skinny woman with weirdly hypnotic eyes in a moldy black gown is waiting for you inside and that she will be very sorry to hear that you lost your way and that of course you must remain there for the night, and she will lead you up a creaking spiral stair by the light of a guttering candle and into a decaying room that would have given Dracula the willies. And then, in the night when you are alone in the dusty bed in the ghastly room, you'll start to hear the noises—the clanking moaning noises, and you will know that something is coming, is creeping out of the shadows—slow, sure, smiling. That's the kind of house it was.

But not if you're an alligator. So Shovel Nose had to miss all this imaginative fun. To him it was just an empty old house where he could always count on finding some mice or rats or other tasty-type things like that.

Well, everything *looked* all right, and even better than that—it *smelled* all right too. In fact, a new smell had been added to the old house since his last visit: a food smell. So he shoved up and went lumbering across the clearing and up the bowed steps, over the sagging gallery, and poked his inquisitive snout through the open door.

It was dark inside, even in the daytime, because of the shuttered windows. And musty too. It smelled of mold and mice and old old wallpaper. And still there was that new smell, stronger now. His little pea-sized brain couldn't quite pin it down because it wasn't at all like the food he caught on the hoof or fin in the swamp.

He entered the shadow-locked foyer and looked around. A troop of mice spotted the reptilian monster and they took off for the wainscoting in a hysteria of haste. Shovel Nose paid no mind to them. His stomach was on the mysterious smell. He waddled through one dank room after another, sniffing and snorfling here and there, and then hauled his ponderous body up the complaining old spiral staircase.

The smell was more pronounced than ever upstairs.

The door of the first room was closed but not on its latch. It shivered open with a rusty screak when he snout-bumped it impatiently.

The room was as black as India ink, cold and clammy. And it had a noise. It hissed softly. It also had a Thing in it…and even though Shovel Nose wasn't pestered by supernatural beliefs, he didn't know what to think when he saw it because he'd never seen such a thing before and his instinct didn't know what to tell him.

It was a pale formless materialization dancing quietly in the black air. It danced toward the door, toward the pop-eyed Shovel Nose who was doing a passing good imitation of a gator statue.

Abruptly a maniacal laugh—which must have been the granddaddy of all lunacy—ripped through the dark old house and nearly stood the poor gator's scuts on end.

"MuuuuuraaAAAHAHAHAAAA!"

Then Shovel Nose's instinct knew what to tell him: *Get going!*

And he did, backing out of there like a hound dog backing out of a hollow log when it comes face-to-tail with a skunk, and he aimed his snout along the hall and followed it for all he was worth, his paws gouging out dusty clots of rotten carpet.

Down the spiral stairs, not using his bandy legs at all now but coming down on his plated belly, banking himself around the turn like a toboggan taking a curve and across the foyer and through the door, down the steps and into the clearing. Then he was in the deep safety of the palmettos and oaks.

And still he didn't know what the enigmatic Thing he had seen was. His gator stability was completely at tilt. The Thing had been cold and damp, his senses had caught that much. But it hadn't smelled, not at all. Alive—but no scent. He snorfed and grumfed irritably and went smashing off to the water prairie to see if he couldn't find a careless fish or a sleepy toad or something like that.

But he hadn't forgotten about the mysterious smell in the old house. He was going to hang around for a while and see what turned up.

* * * *

Way down on Crick Crack Creek Dad Peps was loading his skiff for a gator-grabbing excursion, when Hughie came ripping along the path waving something papery over his fool head. Dad had sent him down to the general store to buy a box of shotgun shells and as far as he could see, Hughie wasn't returning with anything that looked like a box of any kind.

"Dad! Dad!" Hughie cried excitedly. "Lookit what I went 'n bought from ol' Doc Weems with yer ten-dollar-a-gator-hide money!"

Dad looked like a man who has just had his legs sold from under him.

"*From Doc Weems!*" he gasped.

Because ever since old Doc trimmed Dad on the Fountain of Youth, everybody in the swamp (except maybe fools like Hughie) knew that Doc would fleece you out of your last dollar or your prize shoat or your best possum-treeing dog if you didn't throw rocks at him just as soon as you saw him coming.

Dad started looking urgently around for the skiff's stob pole, in order to give stupid Hughie a few lambastings over the head. But Hughie seemed to anticipate the direction of his dad's desire and he hastily shoved a fistful of papery things under Dad's nose.

"Looky, Dad, hit's money. Thirty-some a them! OF Doc said he stopped off at Beebie's Islant this mawnin' and decided to try his luck at diggin' up the ol' colonel's treasure. And guess what he went and found him in the dooryard at the first lick?"

"*What-what?*" Dad panted eagerly. He'd already forgotten about the misplaced stob pole and had his piggy little eyes clamped on the dog-eared old bills Hughie was waving under his quivering nose. Dad went for money the way a bass goes for water bugs.

"All these here paperbacks, is what!" Hughie exclaimed.

Well, all the swampers over the age of two had heard about the legend of Colonel Beebie's treasure, because the tale was even older than Dad—which, to Hughie's mind, put it on a par with Methuselah.

Old Colonel Beebie had lost a leg in the war with Mexico, but even so when the Civil War started he still wanted to go whip the pants off the Yankees. But the Confederate Army said No. They said how could he ride a horse, him all off balance the way he was? And they suggested that he stay home and make himself useful by rolling bandages or somesuch thing.

Well, it had been a great blow to the colonel's honor, and he told them that if they tried to fight a war without his help they were as good as lost, by gum! And what's more their refusal gave him a case of the pouts and he became a crabby old recluse—which is a person who locks himself in the house or in a cave and won't ever come out to say hello to anybody.

So the colonel sold his plantation and took all his money and some carpenters and went out into the muggy swamp and built himself a house on an oak island and never came back again.

It was presumed, of course, that the colonel was long gone dead, because no man could live *that* long. And it was also presumed that his money was out there on that island with his moldy old bones. But even so, treasure seekers were few and far between because the island was far out in the badlands and it had a bad, bad name. There were rumors of lights flickering behind the shutters and thumping noises in the night, as if the poor old colonel's restless one-legged spirit was still hopping up the stairs to his tower to see if the Yanks had arrived yet to steal his money.

Dad's greedy little brain was popping about in his old headbone like a grasshopper on a hot skillet. He grabbed the bills from Hughie and gave them a good close eyeballing.

"Now jest wait a ticky minute here," he said suspiciously. "These fillers don't look much like the paperbacks I git fer my gator hides."

Hughie was appalled by Dad's stupidity. "Dad, you pore ol' fool! You fergit just how *old* these here bills be! These here air Civil War bills, an' money has had a face-liftin' er two since thet time."

"Thasso, thasso," Dad agreed. "But why was ol' Doc willin' to let thirty-some a them go fer a ten dollar?"

"'Cause jest as he was startin' to dig his second hole his foot slipped offn the spade an' he near to brokt his sacarillyact an'—"

"His sack a what?"

"His backbone, Dad. Don't you know nuthin'? And he had to git right off to a doctor an' git hisself hex-rayed er somesuch and couldn't take time to go at no bank an' cash these here old-timey bills in fer new ones. So he sold 'em to me at a loss to hisself. Chuckle!" Dad's wicked little eyes were sharp with speculation. "Hughie boy, y'all know what this means?"

"Well, do I look sappy er somethin'? Course I know what hit means. Means we got thirty-some dollars fer ten, thet's what hit means."

"No, you simple idjut of a boy!" Dad raged vexatiously. "Hit don't mean no sech a thing. Hit means—hek, hek—thet Doc only went an' dug up a small speck a thet air ol' treasure. Hit means, Hughie boy, thet you'n me is goan go dig up the rest a hit!"

Hughie clutched at the air for support. "Dad—Dad!" he wailed. "Tell me yer jest joshin'. You shore cain't mean y'all fixin' to go at thet hanty ol' islant? Why, them hants will take to you 'n me like fleas to a dog!"

"Yes," Dad snapped. "And ifn you don't shet yer biggity mouth I'm goan take to you like a tree failin' on yer pumpkin haid."

Because Dad had those ratty old bills in his hand now and that's all it took to change him from a gator grabber to a treasure hunter.

* * * *

Dad and Hughie had left Crick Crack Creek when dawn's first light lay in cold strips along the eastern horizon and now it was nine a.m. and the sun was already whorling lemon-colored heat over the swamp and they (that's to say: Hughie) were stobbing their skiff across the bonnet-covered surface of Moaning Lake.

"Dad," Hughie's hushed voice matched the somber surroundings, "I reckon I'd like to find me thet ol' colonel's money jest as much as the next filler, but I ain't hankerin' to tangle me with no hants."

"Hughie, will you kindly hesh talkin' like a man with a stop sign fer a brain? I don't give a dead rat what you want. They's treasure a-layin' about thet islant like corn kernels after a hurrycane and I aim to fetch hit home!" Dad reached for his 12-gage and added:

"An ifn any one-leggit hant gits brave an' comes at *me*, I'll purely put so many holes in his sheet he'll catch four kinds a cold when the night drafts git at him. Hek, hek!"

"Mebbe so," Hughie said doubtfully. "But I never yit heered a nobody killin' no hant with'n a twelve-gage er anythin' else."

Neither had Dad; that's why he had nothing more to say about killing ghosts, one-legged or otherwise. He was pure-out worried, but it went against his pride to let on to Hughie. Anyhow, he rationalized, everybody knew that ghosts never came out of a house in the daytime, and he and Hughie were only going to be on the island long enough to dig up a few bags of money. They'd be long gone by the first hint of sundown.

The skiff went plowing into the maiden cane and Dad got out and waited impatiently while Hughie loaded himself down with the 12-gage and a pack with their supper, the fry pan and the spades and the gunny sacks to tote the money in, and a lantern to light their way home. Then Dad went hopping nimbly ahead, using the breathers and log litter for stepping-stones, as Hughie thrashed and stumble-bumbled along in the rear with the load.

Dad's greed had overwhelmed his hant-fears and he let out a war-whoop that put all the cottonmouths into shock.

"Thar's the islant an' hanty house daid a-haid, Hughie! An' ain't thet the dooryard whar ol' Doc found the money? Bet yer mud-stuffed haid hit be! Leggit along here, boy! Stop dawdlin' back thar like a man hooked to a anchor. Fetch me up my spade an' lemme at thet air money ground!"

Well, they went at that patch of earth as if they hated it—spades flashing and dirt flying, and Dad working himself toward a heart attack, and Hughie gasping with heat and near blinded with sweat and so bushed and dizzy he'd sometimes get a mite careless where he was shoveling his dirt and unintentionally let Dad have a spadeful spang in his whiskery face, and then the blue words would come rolling out of Dad like marbles out of a spilled bag.

So by late afternoon the stretch of ground before the shabby old house looked like a battlefield with shell-holes all over the place.

And still no treasure. Not even a rusty old tin can or a dog bone.

"Plague take hit all!" Dad shouted and he heaved his spade down with a slam. "Thet blame money's jest got to be here, somewhere."

Hughie didn't have the strength left to get out of the hole he was standing in. He just sat down where he was like a man in a bathtub without water.

"You reckon they *ain't* no more money than them thirty-some dollars, Dad?" he wondered.

Dad wouldn't hear such fool talk. "Hughie, I clah to *good*ness you be the biggest idjut I ever see! Why, ever'body thet knows enough to come in outn the rain knows thet Colonel Beebie had more'n thirty-some dollars. Why, he had him more money than a bank in a *cee*-ment city! No, they's money here an' I *know* hit's here an' I aim to *find* hit!"

Hughie gave the westing sun a worried squint and said, "Mebbe we best wait till 'nother day. Hit's turnin' on to dark soon. I ain't fixin' to be caught daid on this here hanty ol' islant at night."

But Dad wasn't paying any mind to Hughie. He was cocking his head from right to left as he angrily contemplated the looming house.

"Hughie," he said finally, "ifn they ain't no more money hid in this yard, then the rest a hit's got to be in thet air ol' house."

Hughie looked as if Boris Karloff had just made a grab for him.

"Dad! Dad! You ain't thinkin' what I'm *thinkin'* yer thinkin', air you? 'Cause ifn you air, I ain't *about* to go in thar an' let no one-leggit ol' colonel chase *me* around."

But Dad's greedy look was back in his fierce old eyes again and Hughie knew what that meant. When Dad made up his mind to do a thing *he did it*—even if he had to get Hughie half killed in the process.

"Shet yer wind-slammin' mouth an' climb outn thet hole, 'stead a settin' thar like a leather-haid. I say we goan go in thet house an' find thet money, an' by juckies we shore goan do hit! I tell *you!*"

* * * *

Shovel Nose, flattened and hidden and loglike in the pin-downs, watched Dad and Hughie with great interest. He couldn't understand what they were up to, digging holes in the ground, and now Dad chasing Hughie out of one of them with his spade—but as long as they did it at a safe distance he didn't care.

He watched them head for the old house, both of them walking with tippytoe care as though they were a couple of egg baskets. They slid cautiously through the front door and disappeared.

Shovel Nose waited for a while with blank reptilian patience, and then slithered out of the thicket and into the pocked clearing. The side of bacon that Dad had in the knapsack had been expanding in the gator's nostrils for the past five-six hours. He snatched up the pack in his teeth and switch-tailed out of there, scampering back to the thicket with the pack bumping and scuffing along the ground.

The bacon was very tasty, so he decided to investigate the canned goods too. He tore the first can apart with his teeth and wolfed down the beans, then ripped open the second one and ate the dog food (Dad, not being able to read, never was quite sure just what he was buying when it came to canned food; but it didn't matter because he and Hughie didn't know the difference between dog food and hamburger, and neither did Shovel Nose). He licked his chops with his great slobby tongue and snorfled into the pack for more.

All at once an explosion came booming from the old house, shortly followed by a gosh-awful scream with enough ear-splitting intensity to put a wildcat with his tail in a vise to shame. Shovel Nose yanked his snout from the gutted pack and took off through the scrub for the water prairie. He didn't know what had happened and he wasn't waiting to find out. When Dad and Hughie were on the loose, gators ran first and wondered later.

What had happened was this: when Dad and Hughie got into the deserted house it was darker than ever, now that dusk was coming on, and what with their atavistic superstition about ghostly places, and with half expecting to see the one-legged colonel come flying out of the shadows at them in his sheet at any moment, they were afraid to speak to each other above a sickly whisper. And after they had passed the spooky foyer and entered the shadow-crowding cobwebby-cornered old parlor with its collection of decaying mice-nesty furniture, they were afraid to even breathe.

Then Dad took a silent turn through a ragged drape-hung doorway, and Hughie (who didn't see him do it) didn't, and the first thing they knew they were separated in the huge darksome old house and afraid to say anything about it. After all, there was no sense in *begging* the colonel's ghost to pay attention to them.

So Dad said, in a little wee piping voice, "Hu-hu-hughie?"

And Hughie (by now two rooms away) whispered, "D-d-d-d-dad?"

And nobody, nothing, not even the little mice could hear them.

Dad eased a creaky old door open and edged into a dead-hushed gloomy room and found himself in a library walled with old books, the backs of which were hanging loose from their spines and everything smelling of moldy paper and leather. And right then he was confronted by a ghastly web-draped apparition standing spang in front of him.

It was a terrible sight: the body all scrawny and raggedy and the head all beardy and wild-eyed and gape-mouthed...

Dad said, "*WHAA—!*" and leaped straight up in the air, high enough so you could stand a 12-inch ruler under him and still show space, and when he came down he was carrying his heart in the back of his mouth and he let fly from the hip with the 12-gage, both barrels going *KA-BALOWM-LOWM!* and the ghastly apparition disappeared in a shower of broken glass.

Dad swallowed and his heart slid back down his throat like a slab of raw liver and went thud in his chest. He blinked at the webby remains of the full-length mirror he'd just blown to smithereens.

"Ch-chuckle at myself," he said weakly. "Twelve-gagin' my own reflecting. Hek, hek."

He turned shakily away and walked smack into something which seemed to jangle and jingle and clitter-clatter all over him.

Dad was staring dead into the empty eye-sockets of a grinning skull.

"*EEEEEEYOW!* Hugh-*EEE!*"

Then he got all of himself untangled from that bony old skeleton, and showed how he could spin himself about without hardly even touching the floor, and when he landed he took off like a hard-coated .32 slug…right into the edge of that fool door which he'd left open, his face and chest going *ka-donk!* and if it had been anyone else at any other time it would have knocked him witless or at least broke his nose or maybe a couple of teeth; but not Dad. All it did to him was rebound him about six feet—right back into that blame jinglety-janglety skeleton, which was enough to get him started again.

This time he missed the door and he went out of that room as if he planned on going through walls, and he probably would have too, if any had gotten in his way. Through one room and then the next, and now he was heading for that drape-hung doorway to the parlor—never dreaming that his fool son Hughie, panically looking for a way out, was racing toward the same objective only from a different direction—and *THWHAM!* they collided full front with the drape between them.

Hughie went wobbling away with his legs swinging around like a landsman on his first day at sea during a storm, while Dad took another cross-eyed rebound. But a little thing like a collision with Hughie wasn't going to stop Dad. He got his eyes uncrossed, reversed the direction of his feet, and had another head-down try at that doorway.

"*A skelington!*" he shouted at Hughie in passing. "A one-leggit skelington near to catcht me!"

His fatherly duty done, Dad was long gone down the foyer and out the front door as if someone had yelled, "They're giving twenty-dollar bills away outside!" And he didn't stop until he reached the pocky clearing, where he paused to snatch up his treasure-hunting gear: the fry pan, the spades, the gunny sacks, the lantern…and now where had that blame knapsack got to?

Hughie was coming like a man trying to outrun a cannon ball and nearly making it. He didn't even glance in Dad's direction. He was heading for the thicket and the skiff.

"Hughie!" Dad cried. "Them plaguy hants has gone an' tookt our supper!"

"Laugh at the supper!" was Hughie's frantic advice. "I kin feel thet skelington on the back a my neck!"

Well, there was no stopping Hughie, and Dad wasn't about to be left alone in the clearing with the haunted house for company, so he took off after his spry-footed son and away they went through the pin-downs. And that was no joke either.

It was a mighty soggy, battered, scratched-up Dad, all hurrah blossoms over whiskers with gunny sacks and spades and shotgun and lantern and whatnot sticking from him, who finally reached the inlet where they'd left the skiff in the maiden cane.

Thing was though—there was no skiff.

"D-d-d-d-dad," Hughie spluttered, "folks ain't jest ben joshin' about this here islant. Hit really is hanted!"

"Yeh, yeh," Dad mumbled bleakly. "An' how we goan git offn hit, an' us with no skiff?"

Hughie didn't know. So they simply stood there side by side and stared at the blank space where the skiff had been, as the swamp-misty night closed over them.

* * * *

It hadn't been a ghost that had made off with the Pepses' skiff—it had been their dear old reptilian friend Shovel Nose.

After the gator heard the gosh-awful scream in the haunted house he had taken off for the water prairie and the first thing he saw when he reached the inlet was that skiff. Now Shovel Nose had a thing about skiffs: he hated them, because Dad and Hughie were forever coming along in one to try to catch him. But things were different today; the skiff was alone, unguarded and helpless. He grinned his gator-grin.

He charged snout-down through the cane and rammed the craft head-on, scooting it far out into the bonnet-covered lake. Then he slid into the water and went after the drifting boat like a torpedo.

He had a time for himself. He rammed the skiff and tail-whacked it and came up underneath it to see if he could break its spine, and he kept it up for five-six minutes until he finally had it away out in Moaning Lake. Then his interest was distracted by a bandit-faced raccoon who was washing a frog tasty on a cypress knee.

Shovel Nose let the sorry-looking leaky old skiff drift off by itself and turned back to the island. He had hopes of inviting the 'coon for dinner, frog legs and all.

* * * *

Well, Dad and Hughie were stuck and that's all there was to it. They went back to the clearing and looked at the looming old house and at each other and they didn't know what to say.

Damp night, as black and solid as tar, crowded around them. Somewhere near at hand a limpkin wailed its forlorn lost-child cry, and far out a wolf cut the air with its sad, sad howl, and for a while the swamp was filled with ghostly night music. Then the misty smoke came creeping up from the water prairie and surrounded the two shivering treasure hunters.

"D-d-d-d-dad?" Hughie stammered, "what we goan do now?"

It wasn't Dad's style to remain mute and indecisive when a situation called for action. "*Do?*" he cried peevishly. "Why we goan go inside thet air ol' house an' bed down fer the night, thet's what!"

Hughie looked as if Dad had walloped him with a baseball bat.

"*Go in thet house!* Air you out a yer club-footed mind? I'd as soon spend the night in a barrel a gunpowder with a lit candle!"

"Hughie," Dad said with paternal patience, "do I got a use the butt end a this here twelve-gage on you, er air you goan keep yer door-slaminin' mouth shet when yer dad is talkin' at you? Now ifn you had the sense God give a flea you'd know we cain't spend no night out here in the open. What you want to do—lay down in all this gafocky swamp smoke with nairy even a blankit? And what about all 'em night-prowlin' wolves 'n bears 'n painters 'n cottonmouths 'n gators?"

"G-g-gators?" Hughie made it sound like a spoonful of castor oil.

"I tell you they ain't nuthin' else we *kin* do," Dad insisted. "Anyway, we got the twelve-gage, don't we? And ifn thet ol' skelington goes to git gay with me agin, I'll cold blow him into a boneyard. Him er any other one-leggit hant! I got me a scatter gun in my hands an' I'm a roarin' brawlin' blastin' brass-doorknob chewin' gator-grabbin' corpses-maker from Okefenokee! Thet's what I be!"

"Thet's hit. Dad," Hughie said hopefully. "Pitch hit to 'em! Show them hants who's boss here. Let 'em know we ain't fixin' to have no spooky foolin' around *nohow!*"

"Bet yer two-haided body we ain't!" Dad affirmed with 12-gage bravado and bullheadedness. "Now pick up ourn lantern an' we'll tromp us on in thar an' set thet blame ol' house at rights!"

But somehow Dad wasn't quite as full of loudmouth bluster once he was inside the old house again. Instead of roaring and brawling and blasting, he entered with about as much noise as a snail makes in sand, and he was moving at just about the same rate of speed, too.

"Hu-hughie—let's jest tippytoe upstairs an' find us a room fer the night. No sense in gittin' ol' Colonel's skelington in a uproar agin."

"Yes, l-l-l-let's," Hughie breathed. He was holding the lantern and it was like a little round island of light in a vast black sea. It showed the leprous-looking, paper-peeling old walls leaning ominously toward them, and every time they moved, the black and brown shadows would lurch and expand and shift away as if in flight, and then close in behind.

But they reached the upstairs hall without being jumped by a single ghost; nor did they see or even hear anything that smacked of a ghost, and by then Dad's erratic courage was starting to perk up again. He was even beginning to think that maybe he hadn't really seen a skeleton in the library—maybe he just *thought* he had, because a man's liable to think he sees *any*thing first time he's in a haunted house. Hek, hek.

So they entered a shabby web-strung room which Frankenstein would have crowed delightedly over, and discovered a huge old four-poster bed, all festooned with a rotting canopy, and Dad whispered:

"Stop standin' thar like you'd tookt root to the floor, Hughie, an' close thet door. See ain't they a lock to hit."

"Dad—they hain't even a latch to hit."

"Well, then fetch a chair er somethin' agin hit."

"Dad, they hain't a chair er somethin' in the whole blame room."

Dad's patience had its limits. "Then git out in the hall an' *find* us somethin', you aig-suckin' fool of a boy!"

"Out there? *Me?* By my lone?" Hughie was appalled. "Why I'd jest as soon take the business-end of thet twelve-gage in my mouth an' jump haid-first out the winder withn hit! You want a chair er somethin' so dad-fetchit bad, *you* kin go git hit."

But Dad didn't want a chair or something that bad. He'd made it as far as the bedroom in one piece and he was going to leave it at that.

"I never see sech a boy," he mumbled. "Afeered a hants at his age!"

The old bed groaned and sagged warningly as Dad and Hughie eased themselves onto it, and a thick cloud of throat-grabbing dust billowed from the foul mattress and old, old sheets. But they didn't mind because it wasn't much worse than their own gaggly bed at home. They set the lantern on the floor by the bed, put the 12-gage between them, spread a mothy blanket over them, and settled down for the night.

But not to sleep.

They could hear the old house listening, feel it waiting. To what...*for* what? After a while the lantern burned down-down-down and went out. A black crash of silence covered the room.

* * * *

Outside, the swamp smoke was about a yard high, and for anyone built as close to the ground as Shovel Nose it meant that hunting up a dinner was a waste of gator time. So his stomach just naturally turned to the tantalizing memory of that mysterious smell in the old house, and he went pad-padding across the island to see if this time he could track the elusive smell down to its source.

The old house seemed to be floating on a silent sea of smoke, its yawning front door as ominous-looking as the gate to a graveyard at midnight. But none of this had any effect on Shovel Nose. He had no imagination at all, only an empty stomach.

He slithered into the foyer and snorfed at the clammy black air and was a little perturbed to detect still another new smell, which somewhat overlapped and camouflaged the first. It was the rank odor of Dad's lantern, though Shovel Nose didn't know it.

He hauled his long scutellated body up the stairs to the hall and poked the door to the Pepses' room open with his snout, sniffed at the burnt-out lantern stench, then waddled in quietly to see what was doing. His clawed paws scrabbled softly on the old rug as he worked his way around to the four-poster bed.

When he suddenly heard Dad's whispery old voice right above him, his heart lurched into tilt and he froze from the asymmetrical end of his snout to the tip of his armored tail.

"Hu-hughie?" Dad said in a voice which even radar in the same room might have missed. "You heered somethin'?"

Bet your boots Hughie had heard something, and he was just as tense as a compressed spring. "Mu-mu-mu-mices?" he suggested hopefully.

Dad reached down by the side of the bed to find the lantern—and set his hand on top of Shovel Nose's corrugated head.

"Hughie—I din't see no log in here when we went to bed."

"Log? Dad, you went an' misplaced what little sense you come into the world with? 'Course they warn't no log!"

"Well all I know is they's shore one here now," Dad said hoarsely.

So Hughie fished a match out of his jeans and gave the head of it a snap with his thumbnail and a little ball of flame popped in his hand. And it was right about then that Shovel Nose unhinged his upper jaw and Dad saw that great red-roofed maw with all the jagged teeth rising over the side of the bed and Shovel Nose's angry little eyes sparking at him, and he let out a whoop that would have spooked a spook.

"Eeeeee-*YOW!*"

Hughie took off from the bed in one direction and Dad in another, Hughie getting himself all tangled up in the tattered old sheets and Dad kicking his right foot smack through that blame lantern. And that's the way they went across the room in the dark—Hughie looking like a man fighting a line full of wash, and Dad like a man trying to run with a bucket of broken glass tied to one foot.

Everything came together in the doorway—Dad, Hughie, lantern, and sheets; Dad yelling, "*Me first! Me first!* I'm the dad!" And Hughie yelling, "I don't care ifn yer *ten* dads! Lemme *out* a here!" Then the whole mess disgorged itself into the hall and they stumble-bumbled to the door of the opposite room and, somehow, got it open and blundered into a pitch-black room and got the door closed behind them.

They sagged against the door and made like a couple of fish out of water gasp-gasp-gasping for all their lungs were worth. Then Hughie opened his eyes and realized they were not alone in the room.

"Lord a li'l hoptoadies, Dad! Do you see thet?"

Did Dad *see* it? Well, he hoped to hopping herons he did! Saw it—but couldn't believe it.

A pale formless ghostly creature was dancing quietly in the black air before them. It writhed with rhythmical undulations, its arms and legs coming and going, swirling outward, folding back into its twisting, floating torso. It swelled, it shrunk. A head grew out of the body and expanded. A shapeless gaping mouth formed and stretched to the place where the ears should have been, but there were no ears. Then the mouth swallowed itself and a nose grew and seemed to roll over and down into the glutinous mouth, dragging the huge baleful eyes along. It drifted toward them, the floating writhing arms reaching. It hissed gently.

Well, it was all Dad needed to finish his day, a fat-mouthed gator on one side of the door and a plaguy ghost on the other. He gave that spook a kick in the breadbasket with his lantern-locked foot and the foot and the lantern went *right through the ghost*, just like trying to kick smoke and doing just about as much damage to it.

That was enough for Dad. He didn't care if a whole herd of starving gators was waiting out in the hall (which made two of them, because Hughie didn't care either). They got the door open and they rushed from the black room into the black hall, and they knew Shovel Nose was there somewhere because they heard his jaws slam shut; but Dad knew they hadn't slammed on *him*, and Hughie knew that *he* was still in one piece, and that's all either of them cared about.

They had a dandy race getting out of the old house and once they hit the clearing, Shovel Nose took off for the tules, and Dad didn't stop until he was nesting with a hoot owl in the top branches of a water oak, while Hughie found a hollow log and packed himself into it like a ramrod down a musket barrel.

And that ended the action for the night.

* * * *

Dad was like a rubber ball. You could slam him down hard as all get out but he always bounced back for more. His spirit was as resilient as an elastic band—especially where Shovel Nose was concerned.

He found Hughie in the hollow log the next morning and rooted him out of there by pounding on it with a lightwood stick.

"Stop actin' like a dead man in a coffin an' scrooch out a thar. We got things to do, boy!"

"What?" Hughie wanted to know. "What we got to do, 'cept be gator-bit an' hant-chased an' go hongry?"

"I swar, Hughie, ifn you ain't the most cold-mud-minded boy I ever see! We got a go back in thet house an' find my twelve-gage an' scratch us up some ol' tools to built us a raft with. What y'all thinkin' to do—spend the rest a yer fool days on this blame islant?"

It was too much for Hughie to believe. A cooter bird could have nested in his lower jaw the way it hung open at Dad.

"Dad! Dad! What did you go an' do—leave yer pore ol' brain in thet house last night? I ain't a-dingdang-bout to go back in thet hanty ol' hole!"

"What you worryin' about?" Dad demanded testily. "Shovel Nose's long gone, and—"

"*Shovel Nose?* Great day in the mawnin', Dad, he be the least-est a my worries. What about thet hanty ol' thing we met up with last night?"

"Thet was last night. You got to egg-spect to meet hants in a hanty house at night. But in the daytime them air hants have got to hole up an' sleep. By juckies, boy, ever'body knows thet much!"

"Well," Hughie cried, "ifn ever'body knows hit, then what was we doin' in thar last night? Thet's what I'd like to know! An' what was Shovel Nose doin' in thar? *He* shore ain't no hant."

"Bet yer cotton-stuffed haid he ain't!" Dad raged. "An' ifn he got the gumption to go in thar, then you better believe thet Dad Peps is a-goin' too, 'cause anywhar thet fool gator kin go, *I* kin go! I'm hades on earth, is what I be, an' whar I walk the ground turns to smokin' cinders an' trees shrivel up an' die an' birds fall outn the sky daid an' gators run roarin' in circles snappin' at they own tails! An' right now I'm fixin' to tromp into thet house an' anythin' thet's fool nuff to git in my way had best *BE-WARE!* I tell you!"

Hughie threw his hands in the air and abandoned his fate to the ghosts, because he knew he'd have about as much chance of changing Dad's bullheaded mind as you'd have in kicking a dead horse into getting up and trotting. Dad's pride was at stake. He simply had to show that he had more sand in him than Shovel Nose had.

Dad glared at Hughie to see if any more fool objections were going to come out of his big mouth and, when none did, he turned his fierce old eyes on the gaunt house and shook the lightwood stick at it. "Look out, house!" he yelled. "I'm a-comin' at you!"

And he wasn't the only one…Shovel Nose was also having his third try at the old house.

* * * *

Shortly after Dad and Hughie had creeped in through the front door, Shovel Nose (thinking he had the place to himself) had come out of the scrub and gone around to the rear of the house and slipped in through the kitchen door.

He found some backstairs leading up from the old butler's pantry and he was just starting to ascend them when he heard Dad's crampy voice cut loose with a mouthful of dark blue words practically right over his knobby head.

"*GLAAGH!* Kick myself clear into Christmas! The blim-blam-blankity cobwebbies near to stranglit me! Do they got a have 'em in front a *ever'* door?"

"Why don't you show them ol' webs how the dirt cinders an' the trees shrivel an' the birdies drop daid when you come twelve-gagin' along, Dad?" Hughie suggested snidely.

"Why don't you shet yer sassyfyin' mouth!" Dad yelled.

Poor Shovel Nose didn't know what to think. He switch-tailed himself and went balling into the dining room looking for a hide-hole, and spotted the broken-legged dining table which was canted over on one side and looked like a tent that was about to collapse under its fusty old tablecloth.

He scooted his long scutty body under it and froze, not knowing that at least three feet of his tail was still sticking out in the rear. He listened to Dad and Hughie come closer.

Dad left the backstairs and stepped into the pantry, panning the 12-gage barrels at the clusters of shadows. "All righty," he whispered threateningly. "Jest let somethin' try an' git spry with me now!"

Hughie's eyes ran frantically around in his head as if he expected some supernatural horror to take Dad up on the offer on the spot.

"D-d-d-dad, let's not herd 'em into hit. L-l-let's let sleepin' d-d-dogs lay."

"Well," Dad vowed, "I'll sleep 'em fer good ifn they go to git smarty-pants with me. C'mon, Hughie. Stop shiverin' thar like a man standin' in a barrel a ice water. We got us some tools to find."

"Whar at we goan look, Dad?"

"Downstairs in the cellar fer a starter. Whar else?"

"*In the cellar!*" Hughie gasped, instantly picturing a dank dark dangerous place packed with decaying coffins and rotting skeletons.

"I din't say in the attic," Dad snapped. "Now git them flat-type feet a yorn a movin'. I want offn this blame islant sometime today. Strike a light, boy, an' see ain't thet the cellar door thar."

They were in luck: the door led them down into the cellar. It also led them to a most amazing discovery —a blazing lantern on a table.

"How'd thet git here?" Dad asked warily.

There was a huge old moonshiner's still in one corner of the creepy cellar (but Dad and Hughie were used to finding those things hidden in the swamp), and there was some kind of hand-operated machine like a small printing press. And on the table, near the lantern, was stack after stack of greenbacks. Money, money, money!

"*Heyday!*" Dad crowed. "Hit's the ol' colonel's treasure. Look-it hit, Hughie boy! Hunners an' hunners a dollars! Oh, *I tell you!*"

Well, Dad was like a man possessed. First off he took a running dive spang into the mound of money, then he sat down in the dirt and started pouring the paper bills over his head, chortling and whooping as fast as he could go, and finally he started stuffing it into his pockets and inside his shirt and down his boots and in his hat and…

"Holt on, Dad," Hughie said. "They's somethin' pure-out funny about this here money. Hit's all bran' spankin' new. Hit cain't be the colonel's money. Bet thet air infarnal machine went to make 'em."

"Hughie, you log-haided idjut, I don't give a dead cow how *old* hit be. Hit's *mine-mine-mine!* Oh great day in the mawnin'! I went an' found me a money machine!"

"That ain't all you've found, Grampa," a cold nasal voice said.

Dad and Hughie came to a dead stop. Then they looked around and saw two men—city fellas from the cut of their clothes—standing beside the old moonshine still. One of the men held a snub-nosed .32.

"You've also found yourself neck-high in trouble," the man with the pistol said.

"N-n-n-n-now, fillers," Dad said shakily, "ifn this here money belongs to y'all, why then me'n Hughie shorely wouldn't *dream* a takin' any a hit. Would we, Hughie?"

Hughie shook his head most energetically. Wouldn't dream of it.

"That's big of you," the nasal-voiced man said sarcastically. "What should we do with 'em, Sam?"

The other one, Sam, scowled at the Pepses and said, "Let's lock 'em up in the tower till we're through down here. Then we can decide how to—uh—dispose of 'em."

Dad and Hughie didn't like the sound of that at all, but there wasn't much they could say about it. The man with the .32 said, "Get moving," and Dad and Hughie couldn't think of an argument in the world to give him. They got moving up the stairs.

Dad led the way into the dining room and right off the bat his sharp little eyes spotted that yard of scutty tail sticking out from under the broken table, and nobody had to tell him what it was or to whom it belonged because he knew Shovel Nose from any end.

Well, if you'd told Dad ten minutes before that he was deliberately going to stamp on Shovel Nose's tail, he'd have called you a "borned idjut." Because to his mind stamping on a gator's tail was like sitting on top of a dynamite stick and touching it off just to see where you'd fetch up—and in how many pieces.

But that was before city fellas came along and started pointing pistols at him.

So he did it, because he didn't know how else to get away from Sam and the nasal-voiced man. He just walked by the end of the table and brought his boot down—*whamp!*

For a split second nothing happened.... Then everything happened.

BARRR-OOOM! A great gator roar came booming from under the table and the walls trembled and the plank floor vibrated and dusty pictures leaped from the walls and stick-legged old chairs fell all to pieces, and then gator, table, cloth and all started moving across the room.

"Holy Harry!" Sam yelled. "Do you see *that?* It's a ghost!"

The nasal-voiced man saw it all right, and he saw that mouthful of teeth coming from under the tablecloth too.

"Every man for himself!" he cried, and he and Sam took off for the foyer and the great outdoors, while Hughie proved to himself that he could run backwards just as fast as the other way, and while Dad figured the quickest way out was through a window, and he tried it, headfirst, but forgot about those blame shutters, which ricocheted him back into the room and into four kinds of witlessness.

But it didn't matter because Sam and his partner had made the fool mistake of cutting Shovel Nose off from the door, and now the gator was all mouth and teeth and hot after them. He chased them across the clearing and through the thicket and right into the lap of the Wildlife warden, who was just then landing in his outboard boat.

"Save us! Save us!" Sam screamed hysterically. "It's a ghost!"

"It's a twenty-foot crocodile!" the nasal-voiced man cried.

The warden, who was a big man and nobody to fool with, grabbed them and took the .32 away from them. Then he looked over their trembling shoulders and grinned when he saw Shovel Nose abruptly take off in a new direction.

"Shucks," he said, "that's no croc. That's just old Shovel Nose. He wouldn't hurt anyone—hardly." Then he eyed the two city fellas suspiciously and asked them what they thought they were up to.

"Why—uh—we—" Sam stuttered. "Uh—saaay, couldn't we get in your boat and go out in the lake and talk? That monster might come—"

"No," the warden said firmly. "We're going up to the house and see what's going on around here. All right—march!"

The first thing they saw was Hughie, who was sitting on a stump in the clearing trying to let his lungs catch up to his body.

"Say, Hughie," the warden said, "what's going on, anyhow? I was just coming across the lake, and it sounded like you boys were having a circus out here. Where's that old fool Dad of yours?"

And right then that old fool Dad came stumbling out of the house with bills sticking from every pocket he owned and spilling out of his shirt front, and him yelling, "Hit's mine! Ever' blame dollar a hit's mine! An' the money machine too! *Mine! Mine! Mine!*"

The warden took one hard look at Dad and said, "All right, everyone back into the house. I'm going to get to the bottom of this nonsense here and now."

* * * *

And he did, too. An hour later he had the worried-looking city fellas and the bewildered-looking treasure hunters out in the clearing again, and he said:

"So you see, Dad, these two jokers are counterfeiters. They figured this old house would be just the place to set up their press; first because it's so far out from civilization, and second because they knew all you swampers were afraid to come near the island. But just in case you did—they rigged up the house with a few homemade spooks."

"What about thet one-leggit skelington?" Hughie wanted to know.

"That was simple. They just wired an old skeleton together and hung it from the ceiling. Nothing supernatural about that."

"Yeh, yeh," Dad said, "but what about thet hant upstairs?"

"That's just an old illusionist's trick, Dad. When they found that moonshine still in the cellar they filled it with swamp water, put a fire under it and ran a pipe from the still up to that room and kept the room filled with steam. That was the hissing noise you heard. The ghost you saw was made by a battery light thrown on the steam rising from the pipe. The part of the steam that wasn't lighted was invisible in the dark, so all you saw was the ghost-shape dancing around."

"Ain't hit jest the beatincst?" Hughie marveled. But Dad was plagued by a new worry.

"Then you mean to say all thet money I went an' found ain't—"

"Not worth a dime. Dad," the warden told him. "It's as phony as a liinpkin's wail."

Dad clawed at his beard. "Well, but ain't they a reward er somethin' fer cotchin' countyfuters? I ort a at least git me a—"

"If there was a reward," the warden said, "it would have to go to Shovel Nose. He's the one that caught 'em, as far as I can see."

Dad looked like a mouthful of milk of magnesia. "Well dad-fetchit all, at least I got me them thirty-some dollars a old-timey money thet Hughie went an' bought offn ol' Doc Weems!"

The warden was startled. "You say Doc sold Hughie some money? I think I better have a look at it, Dad." So Dad fished the thirty-some bills from his jeans, and the warden studied the dog-eared old things with interest, saying, "*Tsk-tsk!*"

Dad's eyes were about as anxious as a tail-caught cotton-mouth's.

"What's wrong? What's wrong? Hit's money, hain't hit? Eh? Eh?"

"Y-e-s," the warden admitted, "of a sort. But its value kind of petered out in 1865. It's Confederate currency."

"*Corn-federite?*" Dad fairly howled. "Did you say Corn-fed-crite?" Then his wicked little eyes leaped to Hughie. "Ten a my gator-grabbin' dollars fer—" Even though Hughie couldn't add 2 and 2 or spell cat, he knew the signs when he saw them and he started backing up fast. "Now—now, Dad," he said. "How was I to know, Dad? How was I to—"

A minute later—as Hughie ran a foot race against Dad around the island, Dad chasing him first with a stick and then throwing rocks at him when he couldn't catch up—the warden studied the two woebegone-looking counterfeiters and shook his head, saying:

"Well, it seems like everybody on this island was trying to get something for nothing; and everybody ended up with exactly that—nothing."

Which wasn't quite accurate....

Shovel Nose was upstairs in the old house again and he had finally discovered the source of the mysterious smell. The counterfeiters had been using a fireplace in one of the bedrooms to cook their food, and Shovel Nose had found their portable icebox. Now the icebox was on its side and it was open and empty and a fat ham and a roly-poly roast were on the floor, and Shovel Nose was grinning his gator-grin over them.

And he wasn't the only one that was happy. So were the little mice. Now they wouldn't have to expect him for dinner.

CHAPTER 7

DAD'S DAY OF DAYS

Shovel Nose had been up Crick Crack Creek and he had been grocery shopping and his stomach now contained a dandy collection of bass and frogs and maybe a watersnake or two. So he was ready to crawl off to some secluded spot and sprawl his great scutellated bulk in the sun and enjoy his morning siesta.

He knew just where he was going. He left the creek and pad-padded through a barricade of palmettos to a cypress pond which contained a fallen tree trunk. The trunk ran into the quiet pool like a little wharf and Shovel Nose hauled himself onto it and settled down for his nap, his scooplike snout pointing toward the water.

Even in repose his crooked mouth grinned the inevitable gator-grin.

And he wasn't the only one. Dad, coming belly-down through the bog like a snake, was grinning also. Hek, hek. But Hughie—crawling behind him and lugging a coil of rope you could have moved a house with—wasn't grinning at all.

Dad's bearlike passage had uncovered a colony of flies that were hatching out and still had wet wings, and they simply didn't know what to make of Hughie bearing down on them, and (because they couldn't fly away) they ended up crawling all over his hands and arms and pants.

"*Gaagh! Guk!*" Hughie started making sick noises and he dropped the rope and began pawing the sticky little flies from his body.

"Hughie!" Dad nearly had fits. "How many times I got to tell you not to make a sound when we sneakin' up on a gator? Ain't I ben after Shovel Nose fer years 'n years? An' now you want to go an' spook him away with yer tongue-waggin' trap? This here is the day a days I ben waitin' fer! Now stop beatin' them pore li'l crawlies to death an' listen at me. Here's how we goan do her...."

It was a dandy plan—the way Dad told it. It was shore-fire. They played out the long, long line of tough rope between them, put a slip noose in each end, and Dad took one noose and Hughie the other.

"Now, you take yer end around the far side a the pond. Be shore the rope passes behint thet swamp oak at the end a the pond. Then you wade at one end a the log an' I'll go at t'other. We'll snag him 'fore an' hind, an' let the oak do the holdin' fer us! *Hek! Hek!*"

But Hughie saw a flaw in the marvelous scheme. It had to do with teeth—gator teeth.

"Now holt on a minute here, Dad. Hit 'pears to me I'm gittin' the wrong end a the show. When I git over thar, he'll be aimin' his mouth at *me*. Why don't—"

"Why don't you shet up afore I light into you with a stick!" Dad wanted to know. "I'm the dad, ain't I? I know what I'm doin'!"

Which was true: Dad knew he was keeping himself safely away from that mouthful of teeth. So Hughie resigned himself to a horrible death and sneaked around the pond with his end of the rope, Dad watching him, making sure that the middle span had passed behind the designated swamp oak; then he signaled to Hughie and the two gator grabbers started wading into the shallow pond, coming toward one another, with the unsuspecting gator asleep between them.

It looked good, it really did. Hughie, standing in knee-high water at the far end of the log, was shaking out his noose and preparing to slip it around Shovel Nose's snout, as Dad came cautiously along the rear of the inclined log to noose Shovel Nose's left hind paw.

They were both in place, they were both ready, nothing could go wrong. Hughie looked across at Dad, and Dad—grinning like a devil eating a brimstone breakfast—raised his head to give the nod.

TA-WEEEET!

A tinny whistle shrilled across the swamp like a scream in a haunted house, followed instantly by a peevishly falsetto voice.

"Now, girls! *Girls!* I want you to stay in line like good Beavers. Don't dawdle off the path. Girls!"

Dad's head snapped up. Hughie's head snapped up. Shovel Nose's mouth snapped open.

Hughie looked down into the great toothy-type trap right in front of him and he didn't hang around to admire it because he'd seen it before, but never quite this close before.

"*EEE-YOW!*" He dropped the noose and went high-stepping across the pond, and you would have thought he was running down a nice flat hard highway for the speed he was making.

Shovel Nose was already in motion—scooting down the log with a flick of his tail (which dealt Dad a dandy one in the breadbasket, flipping him boots over whiskers), not noticing in his hurry that his right fore paw had slipped into Hughie's noose. The knot shot home as Shovel Nose rushed for the open water.

The line snapped taut clear back to the oak tree, and around it, and returned to the rear end of the inclined log…which meant that it had snagged on something.

Dad's right foot, in short.

It yanked Dad out of the water and over the log as if he'd been on the receiving end of a power-driven winch. Then it started drag-scooting him along the mud-bank—Dad going in one direction, Shovel Nose going in the other—and Dad yelling:

"*Hugh-EEE!*"

Until he saw himself scooting for all he was worth right for that thick, sturdy oak tree, and then he yelled, "*WAIT!*" And that was the last word he had to say.

He came at that oak like he meant to go right through it. But he didn't. *WHOMP!* Dad slammed into the tree and for a brief moment it looked as though he were greeting an old friend, the way he was hugging the trunk with his legs and arms on either side of it.

Then the line whipped him around the oak like a hoop on a stick and started him good-gosh along into the water again. Dad had nothing to say about it. He had a bemused expression on his whiskery face—eyes crossed, tongue hanging out, nose bent; he was just going along for the ride, a submerged ride. He got to see the fish and the frogs and the mud and all the tough old stones on the bottom of the pool.

Shovel Nose had to pause as he reached the south end of the pond because he found the bank jam-packed with a log litter, and it took some doing to scrabble his great unwieldy body over the barrier. The line went slack and Hughie (mighty brave as long as Shovel Nose was busy at a safe distance) came plunging back into the pond, shouting:

"Here I come, Dad! Holt on! Holt on!"

There was something else Dad could do?

So Hughie unslipped the knot and half lugged, half towed the water-logged Dad ashore. Dad went *ka-plash* on the bank like a big soggy bundle of wash and said "*Blaugh!*" and "*Glauk!*" spitting swamp water and pickerelweeds and bits of lily pads and untasty type things like that.

The Wildlife warden was standing there, along with some other folks, and he had an unamused look on his sun-cured face.

"Well, Dad," he said. "If you're through playing with Shovel Nose, I'd like a word with you."

Dad looked up and thought he'd been knocked sillier than he actually had been. Next to the warden was a skinny old crow of a woman in a Baden-Powell hat, wearing an olive-drab jacket and a baggy skirt to match, with a tin whistle hanging from a cord around her scrawny neck. And next to her, all in a line, and dressed the same way (except for whistles) were six little girls, all going *geeheeheehee* at Dad.

"Do it again, mister!" one of the little girls urged Dad. "Play with the alligator again!"

"Dad," the warden said, smiling benignly at the little girls, "these girls belong to the Beaver Patrol. And Miss Teefle here has brought them into the swamp to observe the natural habitat of the wildlife. I told them I'd show them how gator grabbers work."

"*Issatshoo*—" Dad paused to spit out a pulpy leaf he'd picked up during his trip through the pond, and said it again. "Is thet so? Well, I ain't about to have no blim-blam-blankity brood a li'l—"

Miss Teefle was carrying a parasol (for the sun, you know) and she gave Dad a *bap-bap!* on his soggy head with it, saying sharply:

"My man! My man! Watch your naughty mouth. There are six innocent little lambs here remember." Dad looked as if he'd like to feed the "six innocent little lambs" to the gators, and Miss Teefle too, parasol and all. He kept his naughty mouth closed however. He didn't want to catch another lick on the head.

"Now, Dad," the warden said placatingly. "It wouldn't hurt you to help further the education of the Beavers, would it? You'd like to be a good citizen, wouldn't you? I'll tell you what. If you and Hughie will cooperate, I'll go back to my boat and make out a permit for you to catch a little gator. That way there won't be any danger; and you can even keep and sell the gator. How's that?"

It wasn't much as far as Dad could see, because he always caught little gators anyhow—whenever the warden wasn't around to slap a fine on him for breaking the law; but Hughie had been squatting off to one side all this time, right next to a huge wicker lunch basket which the Beavers had been toting along, and he started making urgent signs before big-mouth Dad could tell the warden off.

"Lemme have a word with you, Dad," Hughie said excitedly.

So, Dad mumbling spiteful things to himself about wardens and parasols and little fool girls, he and Hughie stepped aside to have a whispery confab.

"Dad! Dad! I jest had me a peek in thet air lunch basket and I seen olives 'n jams 'n store-bought bread 'n pears 'n cold meats 'n 'n 'n you know what? *A apple pie!* Thet's what I seen! And what I mean hit's a great round fat type!"

Dad's greedy little eyes were tearing around in his head like two swallows trapped in a barn. He had a thing about apple pies. He went for them the way a bee goes for honey. He gave the warden a sly sidelong glance. "Apple pie," he whispered hungrily. "A *fat*-type apple pie."

"Dad, you reckon ifn we tookt these here Beavers along, they'd see fit to share their lunch an' mebbe give us a slice a thet air pie?" Hughie wondered hopefully.

"A Slice!" Dad went off like a hand grenade. "Hughie, what y'all usin' fer a brain today—a last-year's cooter nest? I aim to git me all of hit! *Hek! Hek!*"

* * * *

Something was following Shovel Nose, stalking him. He was certain of it. Every time *he* moved he heard *it* move. When he stopped he heard nothing. So, wisely, he took a left around a titi clump and cut back on his own trail to surprise the culprit.

Slithering cautiously forward he saw a long skinny tan object stretched along the path. He couldn't understand why a snake would be foolish enough to follow him, but he wasn't going to worry about it. He was growing hungry again anyhow.

He unhinged his jaws and lumbered into a charge. The "snake" immediately started to move again but not fast enough to escape the enraged gator. He scooped it up in his mouth and began to jerk it to and fro savagely—having, in reality, a dandy battle with himself.

By some nameless trend of reasoning this fact began to sink into his brain after a while—one, it didn't taste the way a snake should taste; two, it didn't act the way a fighting snake should act; three, it seemed to have no beginning or end to it, which was mighty strange for the kind of snakes he was acquainted with.

He calmed down and observed the rope. He moved, it moved. He started waddling down the path with the rope slithering along right beside him. Presently the noose in the free end came up and passed him, whipped around the titi clump and disappeared. Shovel Nose kept on going. When he looked back the entire rope was once again stretched out behind him.

So he snorfed and went on his way complacently. The rope didn't seem to be doing him any harm…it was even a friendly sort of thing to have tagging along.

He plodded down to Crick Crack Creek and submerged himself, keeping an eye on the lookout for some fish. He didn't see any—he saw the bottom of Dad's gator-grabbing skiff instead. The black rectangular bottom was passing quietly along overhead. Shovel Nose flipped his tail and took up pursuit.

If Dad had a thing about apple pie, Shovel Nose had one about skiffs. He purely hated them. They meant that Dad and Hughie were coming to give him trouble. He decided to get the first lick in.

* * * *

The warden had told Dad to wait there at the pond while he went back to his motorboat to make out the permit; but Dad had waited only long enough for the warden to vanish among the palmettos. Quickly he had rounded up the Beavers, saying to Miss Teefle:

"He kin cotch up to us later. I know whar they's a li'l ol' gator sound asleep, but we got to leg-hit right along afore he wakes up an' goes fer his noon stroll."

"Well, if you think it's all right, Mr. Peps…"

"Why shore!" Dad assured her. "Now you jest git yerself an' them Beavers into my skiff an' I'll show you some pure-out gator grabbin'."

The Beavers were being girlish and giggly about the whole excursion, and their mouths never shut up for a moment, asking What was that, Mr. Peps? And what, Mr. Peps, was this? And Dad was giving them answers right and left and just being as genial and affable as a good-natured old Santa Claus. He also managed to slip the great lunch basket behind his back and into the bow of the skiff. Hek! Hek!

What he had in mind was so fiendishly funny he couldn't help but chuckle at himself. There was a mud bank down the creek a way where a whole crew of gators sunned themselves every morning. They were small inoffensive fellas, and as soon as Dad landed the skiff and led the Beavers through the maiden cane that gang of gators would take off for the water like a machine gun cutting loose.

There wasn't any harm in those gators, but the Beavers wouldn't know that. They'd leap right out of their Baden-Powell hats when they saw thirty-some gators go to panic all around them.

Dad could just see them jumping and screaming and grabbing each other right now! He could also see himself secretly depositing the lunch basket in a hollow tupelo log he knew of, as he yelled, "Run fer yer lives!" Yessir, it was going to be a kick in the seat!

And right about then one of the little girls pointed to a bird on a cypress knee, and said, "What's that, Mr. Peps?"

"Thet's a limpkin," Dad said offhandedly, not noticing that another little Beaver was scooping up a snake that was drifting lethargically alongside the skiff on the blade of one of the paddles.

"*Oooh*, Mr. Peps! What's this funny-looking snake with the white mouth?" And she swung the blade with its wiggly cargo around to Dad.

"*GAAGH!*" The cry choked in Dad's throat as he saw the "funny-looking" snake coming toward his lap, with the white mouth wide open and the two businesslike fangs ready for angry action.

"COTTONMOUTH!"

Dad went over backwards onto the basket, all legs and arms thrashing, and Hughie who was standing in the rear with the stob pole didn't know whether he should jump overboard or try to climb up the pole, and Miss Teefle was going *tweeeet! tweeeet!* on her fool whistle, while all the little Beavers screamed delightedly:

"Isn't Mr. Peps the *funniest* man?"

The outraged cottonmouth managed to get itself overboard and it squirmed away in zigzag alarm, as Miss Teefle dispatched three of the Beavers to the bow of the skiff to see if Dad needed first aid.

What Dad really needed was a new heart. His old one had nearly stalled completely. He also needed a new plan. That blame whistle of Miss Teefle's had probably scared the gang of little gators away.

But this was Dad's Day of Days and it was just starting; for it was right then that Shovel Nose decided to see if he could break the skiff's spine. He came up from underneath like a malevolent torpedo and he gave it to the boat's bottom boards with everything he had in his ten-foot body.

Beavers and Baden-Powell hats, and Miss Teefle and her parasol, and Dad and Hughie went somersaulting through the air, and it wasn't until Dad was sitting on the mud under four foot of water that he realized something else unpleasant had happened to him.

"Where are the Beavers?" Miss Teefle was wailing.

"Whar is the lunch basket?" Dad yelled as he popped to the surface.

Hughie had the Beavers—or they had him. He was wading around in waist-high water with Beavers by the fistful in his hands and hanging to his belt and clutching him by the hair.

"Dad! Come gimme a hand with these here Beavers!" he demanded.

"Laugh at the Beavers! Whar is thet *lunch basket?*" Dad wanted to know.

Well, the basket was under the bow thwart of the skiff and it was lined with plastic and therefore waterproof. Which was more than the skiff could claim. Shovel Nose's snout had started a couple of the floorboards and the skiff was rapidly filling with swamp water.

Dad saved the lunch basket and watched his skiff settle to the bottom right at his feet. Then he looked up and spotted Shovel Nose's drifting eye knobs observing him from across the creek.

"Thar he be! Thar's the scut-haided horny-tailed riptile thet sunk us!" he fumed. And Miss Teefle (very drenched indeed) was almost as outraged as Dad.

"Oh! The terrible nasty thing! Throw rocks at the nasty alligator, girls. Chase him away!"

Shovel Nose took off in a baffled hurry. Those Beavers were remarkably accurate when it came to throwing rocks. He couldn't understand why the strange little creatures in the big hats should do that to him. He thought that only Dad and Hughie were his enemies. He went away with hurt feelings.

Well, Dad had the lunch basket but he had to have a way to sneak off with it unobserved.

"I'll tell you," he said to Miss Teefle craftily. "We'll find us a tree to hang the basket in, then we'll git on to thet gator hole."

"But, Mr. Peps, why not take the basket with us?"

"Naw, naw. The goin's too rough. Hit'll jest holt us back. Hughie! Stop settin' thar like a bag a wet wash. Fetch up the spade 'n axe from the skiff."

So, in a stand of tupelos, Dad selected a tree with a broken branch and hung the basket to it by the handle. Then he slipped Hughie a sly wink and led the way into a thicket of paint-root and titi that was so almighty dense it would have given a bear pause for consideration.

But the Beavers loved it. It was a regular jungle. Their gab-gabby voices piped and squealed and chatter-chattered until Dad began to suspect he was leading a flight of magpies.

He brought them out in a lonely stretch of badlands. There was a large, shallow, boggy pool, and fronting the pool was a slope-sided bank of dirt. Dad led the Beaters along the foot of the bank to a small dark opening, cautioning them to be very quiet. The Beavers could hear the gator breathing in his sleep inside his hide-hole.

"Now here's the way we catch 'em," Dad said importantly. "Fust off we [he meant Hughie] cut us some stakes and we plant 'em like bars acrost the opening of the hole. Then we [Hughie again] dig up the roof a the cave an' we got the gator caught in a pit! Hughie! Why you standin' thar like a man waitin' fer a train? Git a movin' with thet air axe. These here li'l gals want to see some gator-grabbin', is what!"

So Hughie went to work with the axe, chopping sticks for the bars, and the Beavers took turns on the spade digging up the ga-tor's roof, while Dad—just as crafty and sly as a fox near a hen-house—slipped off into the thicket unobserved. Hek! Hek!

* * * *

Two things went wrong in two different places. The first hap-pened at the gator hole....

Dad had been right when he said the gator was little, but this one was so small he was less than a yard. And when he suddenly saw his roof coming off over his head he went into a panic and scooted between the bars Hughie had planted without any trouble at all.

He headed for the pond, and the Beavers went right after him with cries of delight...running so fast and excitedly that three of them were well into the center of the pool before they realized that something was wrong. They looked down and saw that they were standing in only a foot of water, yet they couldn't seem to move their feet.

Hughie started into the pool yelling like a madman.

"Come back! Come back! Thet's a sinkhole!"

TA-WEEEET! TA-WEEEET! Miss Teefle blasted away on her whistle imperiously, as Hughie managed to grab up the three Beavers who were closest to the shore.

"Girls, Girls!" Miss Teefle called to the other three. "Come back this instant! Didn't you hear Hughie tell you not to go in there? Come out immediately!"

"Mizz Teefle, ma'am," Hughie cried, "they *cain't* come out. Thet's a sinkhole...*quicksand!*"

The second thing happened near the stand of tupelos....

* * * *

Dad was skirting the worst of the thicket and coming along on his spry old legs through the palmettos when he ran onto his rope, noose and all.

"What's this?" he wondered, and he picked it up by the noose. "Ain't this my rope? How'd hit fetch up way out here?"

Right then the rope gave a little tug in his hand. Dad gave it a tug back. The rope replied again. Dad glared at it peevishly and put his hand through the noose to get a good purchase on the rope. He went tug-tug-tug at it. The rope went tug-tug-tug right back.

"I'll git me to the bottom a this!" Dad vowed.

He started following the rope through the palmettos. He followed it right into the stand of tupelos. Then he stopped. Then he went bug-eyed. Then his lower jaw dropped open.

Shovel Nose was standing on his stumpy hind paws, his fore paws against the tree with the broken branch supporting his huge body. He had just taken the handle of the lunch basket in his jaws. Then he turned his head and saw Dad standing at the other end of the rope.

Dad swallowed as he suddenly saw a beautifully clear picture of exactly what was going to happen next.

"Now—now—now wait a durn minute, you blame riptile—"

Sss-ock! The noose shot home on Dad's wrist as Shovel Nose took off with the lunch basket bouncing and banging in his jaws. And it wasn't all that was bouncing and banging. Dad was coming after him like a tin can tied to the tail of a scared dog. He was going to have another guided tour of the swamp whether he wanted it or not.

"*WAIT—WA—OOP! UGH! WAIT—WAIT!* Not in the gafocky thicket! Not in the—"

But Shovel Nose wasn't about to wait for man or beast. He was dead-set on outrunning Dad and he didn't care where he went or what he did to do it. The thicket was handy and maybe there would be water on the other side of it, and so he took it.

And so did Dad, who didn't have much choice in the matter.

Jobbity-jop, jobbity-jop, over the root-crossed branch-tangled stone-pegged marshy turf came Dad, first on his right ear, then on his nose, next on his seater, now on the back of his head. *Bump-bumpity-bump* across a log litter, and then *yay-hey!* headlong into a jungle wall of bay and amber berries and yellow jessamine and scarlet ivy trumpets and pink hurrah blossoms, and when Shovel Nose lumbered into the badlands Dad looked like a mobile flower display.

Just a minute before, the warden had finally caught up with the Beavers, and when he saw three of them in the pond he knew exactly what had happened and he immediately started to cut some lengths of cane. He only hoped that the pieces would be long enough to reach the little girls. They were pretty far out.

And right then Shovel Nose and his friend arrived on the scene.

The warden had no idea what Dad thought he was doing slamming along on the end of a rope tied to a gator, but it was plain to see that Dad's unwanted presence there was simply spooking Shovel Nose out of his few wits.

"Look out, Hughie!" the warden yelled. "You're cutting Shovel Nose off from the water!"

Hughie took one look at the reptilian locomotive and its bouncing caboose bearing down on him and he started snatching up Beavers and shouting, "Run, Mizz Teefle! Dad's ben hurrahin' Shovel Nose agin, an' thet gator's pure-out mean!"

The warden forgot about cutting cane. He watched Shovel Nose scurry for the water. The gator's path was clear now, and if he saw the three little Beavers standing in the pond he probably took them for cypress knees in his excitement.

In he went, and Dad too (complaining about it every jolting foot of the way), and then as he leveled his great scutted body along the surface he spotted the three Beavers standing in front of hint and he tail-hitched himself onto a new course, swinging Dad around in a wide foamy arc. The warden started running, shouting:

"Grab that rope, girls! Grab the rope quick!"

They didn't. They grabbed Dad instead as he came scooting by. They just loved good old affable Mr. Peps. Shovel Nose kept right on tail-kicking for the far shore, and the Beavers rode Dad out of the pond like a paddleboard. And if Dad had anything to say about this aquatic hitchhiking he had to say it underwater.

Shovel Nose got hung up in a barricade of cypress knees, which to a gator are just about as treacherous as a tank-trap is to an army tank, especially if he has a waterlogged weight tied to his tail and jammed among the breather stumps.

It took the warden a while to run around the pond, and by the time he made it Shovel Nose was in a testy mood. He thrashed his tail and backrolled his eyes. He didn't know whether he should retain his grasp on the basket (so the warden couldn't take it) or drop it and take a bite at the warden—who was now approaching him with a knife in his hand.

"Easy, old fella," the warden said soothingly. "You know me. I wouldn't hurt you." And with one quick deft slash he cut the noose from the gator's leg, saying, "Shoo, Shovel Nose! Off you go!"

Which is just what Shovel Nose did, lunch basket and all. And he didn't waste any time about it either, because Miss Teefle was going *Taweeet!* on her whistle again, and shouting:

"Bless that wonderful alligator! *He saved the Beavers!*"

And the Beavers themselves started shouting around the pond. "Rah-rah-rah, *Shovel Nose!*"

The warden went over to see how Dad was doing. At the moment all Dad was doing was disgorging a quart of swamp water from himself.

"Well, Dad, it looks like Shovel Nose is the hero of the day," the warden said warmly.

Dad had nothing to say about it...not out loud, that is; because he was afraid that Miss Teefle would come after him with that blame parasol again if he did. He contented himself with saying, "*Glaak!*" wetly.

CHAPTER 8

THE DANDY DEADFALL

She was the most beautiful creature in all Okefenokee—in Shovel Nose's eye. She was scut-bodied and armor-tailed, had teeth like stob poles and a mouth like a cave. She was nine feet long and she was all gator. Shovel Nose was completely enamored of her.

The she-gator had set up housekeeping in a small cypress pool on the west end of a swamp island. Shovel Nose had his hide-hole on the east end. The high land was honest, solid earth and it was thickly crowded with pine and oak and palmettos, with pink hurrah blossoms blazing up like flames under the trees. The island itself was encircled by a dense pin-down thicket, log litter, and a watery bog. Only a fool or a gator or a gator grabber would want to go there.

The she-gator was friendly enough in a slightly standoffish way: at first she unhinged her ponderous jaws and hissed threateningly at Shovel Nose's clumsy advances, and then—when he insisted upon being neighborly—she pivoted her bulky body and gave him a lick with the flat of her laterally swinging tail. But Shovel Nose was a good-natured sort; he grinned his gator-grin and bumped the point of his blunt snout against her burly shoulder and even gave her paw a playful nip or two. And, in the end, the she-gator decided that the strange gator with the asymmetric snout meant well.

The cypress pool was too small for two full-sized gators to frolic in, so they waddled under the pin-downs on their bellies and went down a maiden-cane channel to a water prairie.

First they chased a furiously frightened cottonmouth into the log litter, then they had a game of tag with two clownish otters (until the otters were distracted by a distant water turkey and scooted off to harass the soggy bird), and finally they encountered a school of bass and decided to go shopping.

They enjoyed a tasty fish dinner, swallowed a few pebbles to help their digestion, and then the she-gator headed for home. It was time for her sunbath and nap.

She sprawled on a fallen cypress spanning her small pool, gave a snort of contentment and closed her eyes. Shovel Nose stood on the mushy bank and cocked his head at her. Then he began "grunting up." But she paid no attention to him at all. There was a time for play and a time for sleep; every gator should know that much.

So, good-naturedly, Shovel Nose switchbacked himself and went waddling across the island for his own pool. The path he followed was very narrow and shadowy like a pale green underwater passage. It was walled with wild flowers, palmettos and swamp oaks, and it had once belonged to the deer, bears, and wild pigs. Now it was Shovel Nose's exclusive property. However, he was in such a jovial mood that he didn't even complain when a fool poor-joe bird hopped into his path and began scolding him furiously about something or other.

It had been a good day, a very good day indeed. Shovel Nose pad-padded happily on, letting the poor-joe bird frantically flutter out from underfoot best way it could.

The jungled path closed behind the gator and the swamp stillness slid back into place. For a moment there was no sound, no movement at all. Then, with infinite care, a palmetto frond by the path was shoved quietly forward like a small green door opening in a long green wall, and a scraggly-bearded sly-eyed face peeped out.

It was Dad chortling softly to himself.

"*Kek, kek.* This time, you scut-sided riptile, I purely got you cold!" Then he closed the frond on his wicked little eyes, which sparked like two crumbs of glass, and slipped silently away.

* * * *

It was in the waiting hush of evening when Dad returned to the pine island. He was sitting—as usual—in his battered old skiff, and his fool of a son—also as usual—was working the stob pole.

The going was as mean as a bear with his paw in a trap and Hughie was fairly working himself into a lather. First there was the dad-blasted water lettuce, just as thick and grabby as fish hooks; then the log litter and cypress knees, and they were about as friendly as tank-traps; and finally the good-gosh pin-down thicket. But Dad was as helpful as could be. He called encouragements to Hughie from the stern.

"Hughie! You bat-blind idjut! Mind thet breather thar to leftward! You lookin' to upset us er somethin'?" And, "Thet's hit! Pile us spang into the blame log litter! Rip the bottom boards outn the skiff! You beanbag-brained fool of a boy!"

"Dad," Hughie said, with maybe just an edge of temper to his clacky voice, "I don't reckon hit ever entered thet space you got 'tween yer ears to spell me a mite on this here pole? I'm so pure-out bushed now my tongue is near to draggin' in the water."

Dad was in an amiable mood—his gator-grabbing mood. He said, "Good! See kin you bait a fish with hit fer our supper. *Kek! Kek!* Now shet yer sassyfyin' mouth an' look alive. Yander's the islant."

It was the end of the road for the skiff. The pin-down barrier stood between the two gator grabbers and the high land. Dad rubbed his grimy palms together and hopped nimbly overboard, sinking knee-deep in the bracky water.

"Fetch along the rope, boy," he ordered. "I'm fixin' to snag me the king a gators!"

They clawed and hacked their way through the pin-downs (Hughie in the lead doing the clawing and hacking, Dad wading behind), and into the titi and paint-root and palmettos, and up to the sequestered path.

"Here's what we'ns will do," Dad said, and promptly sat himself on a bit of oak stump—which meant that he'd do the talking and Hughie would do the doing.

"We'll tie us a slip knot in thet air rope an' we'll clumb thet there oak tree an' tie t'other end around thet there fat-type limb a-standin' over the path. Then we'll drap the noose right down over the path an' we'll decky-rate hit with leaves an' sech so cain't no gator tell what hit is, an' then when ol' Shovel Nose comes a-footin' hit down the path to pay his gal a call, he'll kindly poke his haidbone spang into the noose an' we'll lasso him!"

"*Lasso* him!" Hughie cried incredulously. "Dad, Dad, how we goan handle a ten-foot mouth-snappin' tail-kickin' gator in a lasso?"

Dad had an answer for everything. He stood up and handed Hughie a long, sturdy stick. "Simple enough," he said. "After the pore stupid gator pokes his snout into the noose, *you* goan step out a hidin' and lambast him proper 'n peaceable with thet air club."

"*I'm* goan lambast him? Well, what *you* goan be doin'?"

There was no doubt in Dad's mind about what he was going to do: he was going to keep out of the way of that mouth-snapping tail-kicking ten-foot gator. "I'm goan be up in the tree mindin' t'other end of thet rope," he said. "Somebody got to do her, don't they?"

"Yeh, but why cain't *I* be up thar a-mindin' the rope, an' *you* be down here a-lambastin' Shovel Nose?" Hughie wanted to know.

Dad was patient with his simple son; he explained it this way:

"'Cause I'm yer dad an' I'm a-tellin' you how we're a-goan do hit, is why! Now shet thet barn-door mouth a yorn an' git a-movin' with thet air rope, afore I take thet stick back an' clop you over the haid with hit!"

And so—mumbling a mouthful of blue words—Hughie tied a noose in the rope and climbed the oak, tied the free end to the branch over the path, and came down and camouflaged the noose with sprigs of leaves. Then he paused to contemplate his work. There was no doubt about it—if Shovel Nose came along the narrow path he was bound to run his snout smack through the noose, and the very momentum of his great body would cinch him up proper.

"Looky here, Dad," Hughie worried, "hit's gittin' on to dark. I ain't fixin' to set me out in this buggy ol' swamp all night a-waitin' on some fool gator thet's off sleepin' in his hide-hole somewheres."

"Hughie, will you kindly stop frettin' yer pore ol' brainbox? I know thet gator backwards. He's a night prowler is what he is; and I'll bet yer suspenders he'll be along here shortly to see don't his gal friend want to go huntin' with him."

Dad gave his hands another energetic scrubbing and trotted over to the oak. He looked at it this way and that, trying to discover just how Hughie had climbed the blame thing.

"Hughie!" he cried peevishly. "Don't jest stand thar like a rag-haided scarecrow in a field! Come hep yer dad up the tree. By juckies, boy, do I got to do *ever'*thin'?"

The dark crept in on little cat feet and settled down quietly for the night. Then the vast bog started to smoke, and presently the swamp mist began to unfold itself over the island, slow, sure, silently.

Dad sat on the limb overlooking the smoky path with his back against another branch just behind him. In his lap he held the coil of rope that he and Hughie would use to tie Shovel Nose with after Hughie had pacified the monster with the club.

Suddenly he felt the branch at his back give a little; then he heard a rustling of leaves. Dad looked around and saw a formless silhouette sitting in the dark above. A glinty pair of eyes stared back at him.

"Hughie!" Dad hissed angrily. "Have you gone out a yer pea-pickin' mind? What air you doin' up here in this tree?"

"*Rrrrrrowrrr,*" the silhouette said throatily.

"Hu-hu-*huu*ghie?" Dad asked tentatively.

"*RRRRRROWRRR!*"

Dad was quick about these things; he could tell the difference between Hughie in a tree and a wildcat in a tree anytime. "*Hugh-EEE!*" he bellowed. "*HEP YER DAD!*"

Then the wildcat went for Dad and Dad's balance went all to pieces and down they came, wildcat clinging to the top of Dad's head, and leaves and twigs and the fool coil of rope tangling after.

"Hugh—"

WHOMP! Dad hit the ground like a bag of sand and the wildcat was long gone like something fired from a gun.

Hughie couldn't see for dark and swamp smoke, but there was nothing wrong with his hearing. He leaped from behind a tree with the long, sturdy stick raised over his head and rushed into the path, yelling:

"Holt him, Dad! Holt him! I'm a-comin'! I'll lambast him!"

Whamp! Whamp! Whatnp! Three lambastings on top of Dad's head.

"*HUGHIE!* What air you *doin'?* This's *yer dad* yer lambastin'! You brain-loose club-haided fool!"

Hughie paused in consternation. He peered down into the swirling swamp smoke, then reached into it and felt around until he grabbed Dad's beard. He gave it an inquisitive tugging.

"Dad? Ain't you Shovel Nose, Dad? Whar's ol' Shovel Nose at?"

It was the wrong time to ask the question—Shovel Nose was standing ten yards down the smoky path blinking his startled eyes at the vague, shadowy movements before him. He recognized Hughie's clacky voice and Dad's crampy one, and he reasoned that the two gator grabbers were trying to "cut him off." He cracked open his jaws and filled the swamp with night thunder.

"*BAARRR-OOOM!*"

It was the old, old familiar sound to Dad and Hughie, and Hughie took off without hardly even letting his feet catch up to him, while Dad shot up like a jack-in-a-box and started to leg it— but in the wrong direction, nearly running himself right into Shovel Nose's yawning mouth—got himself turned around and went sprinting down the path, putting his left foot unwittingly through that blame noose, and the rope let him take three-four fast steps more, then the knot slipped home on his ankle, jerking his spindly legs clean out from under him.

Hack he came, digging a furrow in the path with his face, swinging like a pendulum on a granddaddy clock, and he knew what was waiting for him at the other end of the swing—gator teeth.

Spluttering out dirt and whiskers, Dad flipped himself over and skinned up the rope hand-over-hand and into the oak quicker than the wildcat could have gone scat.

Shovel Nose closed his mouth and snorfled through the swamp smoke. He couldn't understand what had happened to Dad. Gone. Simply gone. He waddled on down the path greatly perplexed.

An unpleasant welcome awaited him at the cypress pool. The she-gator was awake and she was in a terrible temper. She had been sleeping in her hide-hole when suddenly a wild-eyed Hughie had come crashing through her pond and practically into her cave; and before she could even get her jaws open to give him a good bite, Hughie had tromped on the tip of her snout and gone up over the bank and disappeared.

The she-gator didn't know anything about Dad and Hughie and their gator-grabbing activities, and the violent encounter with Hughie had upset her gator stability shockingly. Now, unreasonably, her little pea-sized brain associated Shovel Nose's arrival with Hughie. She went after the poor innocent gator in a perfect fury—hissing, slamming her jaws, *barrrooming* up a storm.

Shovel Nose retreated for home in a hysteria of hurt and bewilderment. Back down the path he lumbered with his snout low to the ground, never knowing that at one point a panting, dirt-chewing, rope-burned old gator grabber was sagging in the branches over his head.

You had to say this for Dad: he never knew when to quit. Back he came to the island two days later, the fierce light of combat still a-gleam in his eye.

"They wasn't nuthin' a-tall wrong with my idee," he insisted to Hughie, as Hughie stobbed the leaky old skiff toward the pin-down thicket. "To catch him on thet pathway is jest as foolproof as a lock on a door. Oh, I'll git him this time, jest as shore's mud's soft! All I got to do is go at hit with a new type a trap."

"What would thet be, Dad? What type a trap?"

Dad looked slyly pleased with himself.

"A deadfall. The slam-bangin'est deadfall you ever seed!"

Hughie looked baffled. "Y'all fixin' to deadfall Shovel Nose *daid*?"

"No, I ain't fixin' to deadfall him daid, you two-haided thinkless type a boy! How many times have I gone tolt you I want him *alive* to sell to them air tourist centers? Now hesh up thet fly-trap you call a mouth an' fetch along them ropes an' thet wood-chop-pin' axe. I got me a catch-em-alive type a deadfall to build!"

Hughie knew what that meant—and he was right. Dad found a half-grown honey bear working an old bee stump and he chased the round-rumped little fella away, sat himself on the stump and proceeded to gum up some honeycomb. Hughie went to work with the axe under Dad's wax-mumbled directions. He chopped up thirty-some branches as thick as his skinny wrist, and then—Dad issuing instructions like a general—he started to construct a long, narrow, not-too-tall cage.

Finished at last, Hughie plopped into the sawblade grass like an old newspaper no one wanted, all gaspy and soggy from exertion and heat. "Thet what y'all had in mind, Dad?" he panted.

Dad wasn't at all tired. He hopped right up from his stump and trotted over to inspect his masterpiece. "Hit's a pure-out dandy, thet's what hit is!" he crowed. "Hit's the best durn deadfall I ever built me! Bet I could catch me a ellyphant in hit—leastways a small one—let alone thet dent-haided scoop-nosed blame gator!"

He nudged the prostrate Hughie with his foot.

"Great day in the mawnin', boy, why you lazyin' round down thar in the weeds? We shorely got us some work to do! Heyday, Hughie! I kin purely see hit now—"

So could Hughie: he could see Hughie doing more back-breaking work with the monstrous cage. He groaned.

"I kin see you'n me at one a them tourist centers," Dad yammered happily on, painting a glowing dream future, "an' we got Shovel Nose inside this here very cage an' you'n me is standin' outside jest a-sellin' tickets hand over fist to them air tourist-type folk an' them folk is a-comin' from all over the hull world jest to see the biggest, slam-bangin'est gator in captiv'y! That's what I see!"

"You see anythin' in thar about *you* helpin' me to catch Shovel Nose in thet cage?" Hughie wanted to know.

"Shet yer impiddy mouth afore I poke the axe-haid in hit," Dad said in a fatherly way. "Now git ofn yer scater an' hep me tote the cage. You 'spect yer pore ol' dad to do all the work by hisself?"

They lugged the contraption to a wide piece in the gator path and set it down under the overhang of a squatty old live oak. Then Hughie lashed a rope to one of the top bars of the cage at both ends, making a giant rope handle. Next he tied another rope to the center of the handle, and then he skinned up the tree with it and he and Dad (who was still down below and giving more lip-service than help) tugged and hauled the cumbersome, cranky old cage into the air, and Hughie anchored the key rope around a branch.

Dad looked up at the huge cage hanging a foot above his head and gave his thigh a resounding slap.

"Hughie, you hop out a thar now an' root up some bresh to commyfloge our deadfall. By juckies, boy, I'm shore goan nail him this time. I kin feel hit in my bones!"

Hughie did as he was told and then asked, "Dad, y'all want me to hep you up the tree now?"

But Dad wasn't about to share a tree with another wildcat. This time he was going to keep his flat feet on the ground where they belonged.

"Tell you, Hughie," he said diplomatically, "reckon we'll go turnabout. You keep in the tree, and I'll hide me down here some-wheres. Now, boy, I want yer to listen at me good. You set thar with yer Barlow knife ready, an' when I give the word, you let her rip. And then—*WHANG! BANG*—down comes the deadfall an' knocks ol' Shovel Nose all to gafocky! *Kek-kek*. Oh, what a dandy day this will be!"

* * * *

It was also a long day. Hours crawled by like sleepy turtles, but no Shovel Nose. The pesky skeeters came though, and all the nameless little crawlies that lived among the grubby roots, and a whipcoach snake mistook Hughie's leg for a limb of the tree and nearly scared him into a headfirst tumble. And still no Shovel Nose.

"Dad—" Hughie risked a call down to Dad, who was squatting in a hurrah bush fighting a quiet little war with the crawlies that were infiltrating his pant-legs. "You reckon mebbe Shovel Nose gone left this here islant?"

"Course he ain't gone left hit! Not so long's thet gal-gator lives here. Bet he's over to her pond right now. You'll see!"

"Yeh—but, Dad, what ifn *she's* gone an' moved? After that ruckus we kicked up around here night afore last, I'm some surprised if even a cooter bird would stay."

Hmm. There might be something in what Hughie said. Dad gave it some thought by giving his beard a mauling. The more he tugged and fretted the more he worried, until finally he knew he couldn't sit there a minute longer without knowing for sure.

"Hughie, you sit tight. I'm jest goan sneaky-foot over to thet gal-gator's pond an' take me a peek."

Hughie watched Dad go tippytoe down the path like a man stepping through eggs, and then resettled himself in the old oak. He was hot and bored and skeeter-pestered, and now some sticky tree worms were getting in the habit of dropping down the back of his neck. He kindly wished that Dad and Shovel Nose would get this fool business over with.

Abruptly—violently—it seemed his wish was coming true. Somewhere down the path he heard Dad's shrill old voice split the swamp silence like a hammer through a pane of glass.

"*EEE-YOW!*"

"Now what's he gone an' done to his fool self?" Hughie wondered.

"*HUGH-EEE!* Do somethin', boy! I'm near to bein' gator-et!"

Hughie angled himself around a limb and took a look down the path and saw that Dad wasn't just joshing: he and the gator were coming good-gosh along for all they were worth—Dad in the lead but only by inches, and the gator's mouth so wide open and close behind him that Dad looked like a man running out of a cave lipped with stalactites.

Hughie got all panicky. He didn't know what to do. He looked at the Barlow in his hand and then did the only thing he could: he cut the rope and let the deadfall rip.

PALOWM! Down it came with an explosion of dust and dirt and leafy branches, and Dad and the gator disappeared from the path as though they'd been swallowed alive in one gulp. Hughie dropped from the tree and started pawing through the leaves to reach the struts of the cage.

"Hi, Dad!" he shouted excitedly. "We went an' cotched ol' Shovel Nose, Dad! …Dad? Whar you be?"

Dad was on his knees and he was knocked slightly witless from the blow the deadfall had given him when it landed on top of his frizzly head. His eyes were wandering about like two fish in a bowl.

"Yeh, yeh," he mumbled. "We caught us ol' Shovel Nose. A dandy day, like I said. A dandy, dandy day…"

Then he woke up with a rush and realized a trifle late that something was wrong, very very wrong. He wasn't outside the cage looking in at the gator: he was inside looking out at Hughie.

"Hughie! What have you gone an' *done*, boy! You got *me* in the deadfall with the gal-gator!"

"*BARRR-OOOM*!" right in Dad's ear, and it was like having his head at the mouth of a cannon when it slammed off. His equilibrium went all to pot and he vibrated around like a man holding a live wire and looked smack down the she-gator's throat.

You had to give Dad credit for the spryness he showed in emergencies. He couldn't go forward, and there was no way of going *around* the gator, so he went over her. Right up the end of the cage and onto the underside of the top bars he went and started aping his way to the rear.

The she-gator didn't have enough room to get herself turned around to go after him, so she had to settle for what she could do with her tail. She thrashed it to and fro, banging it from one side of the cage to the other, getting in a lick at Dad's hanging bottom each time; and Dad, upside down like a fly, yelling, "Hughie! *Git me out a here*, you thumb-haided fool!" And Hughie scrabbling all over the cage, chanting, "Holt on, Dad! Holt on. Dad!" and not doing a thing to get Dad out. And all the while the frantic gator thundering one *baarr-oom* after another.

Shovel Nose had been pouting around in his boggy pool for two days feeling mighty sorry for himself and disgruntled with the swamp world in general: but the moment he heard the she-gator's roar he forgot all about the unjust way she had treated him. He came scrambling out of the water and onto the bank and leveled himself down the path like a torpedo speeding for its target.

And it was just about this time that Hughie had a brainstorm.

"When I give the word, Dad—drap like a rock 'n roll outn thar!"

He scampered to the rear of the cage, dropped to his knees and started to lever the end of the deadfall upward; and it was a chore, what with Dad's hanging weight and that blame gator tail swishing back and forth in his face; but he was getting it—slow, sure…

A long scut-green cigar-shaped body came lumbering into view—not looking right or left, the blunt, scooped snout leading the way like a warhead, the little furious obsidian eyes hard on the cage that held the she-gator captive. And that was the way Shovel Nose struck the forward end of the deadfall, snout-on and with ten feet of heavy-plated muscled gator behind the punch.

The cage—already raised in the rear—leaped upwards and backwards. One instant Hughie was kneeling with the end of the cage nearly over his head, and the next instant he was kneeling in the same place with the cage all over him and with Dad yelling blue murder in his lap.

The she-gator came scrabbling out from under the forward end of the cage and looked at Shovel Nose with an expression like a question mark. Shovel Nose grinned his gator-grin at her. Then he started grunting-up—showing off just a little.

Well, it came down to this for Dad and Hughie: as long as they stayed inside the cage they were safe. So Dad had a plan. He got at one end and Hughie at the other, and they lifted the cage and walked it that way.

Trouble was though, after a while Dad got the idea that Shovel Nose was trying to herd them. The fool gator kept making little rushes at their feet, turning them more and more toward the south side of the island.

With the she-gator tagging amiably behind, Shovel Nose kept the game up until he had the two caged men situated on an oozy mud-bank which fronted a dismal slough. Then he seemingly lost interest in the sport. He grunted suggestively to the she-gator, and they waddled off together to go see if they could find the two playful otters in the water prairie.

"All righty!" Dad raged spitefully. "Jest lemme out a here, an' lemme git my hands on my twelve-gage an' I'll pump so much lead into thet carnsarn gator, he'll sound like a bag a ball bearin's when he walks!"

"Dad! Dad!" Hughie hissed. "You hear thet gruntin' comin'? Hit kind a sounds like—*gators*, don't hit?"

Dad shut his cranky mouth and glared around at the thicket and the slough. All at once he started yelling.

"Why, thet wuthless, scut-haided, four-leggit idjut went and parked us spang in the middle of gator ground!"

EPILOGUE

It was a long night and a buggy one too. And when the new dawn cracked over the cypress-bound horizon it shed light on a remarkable scene—a knock-kneed, sticky old cage on a cold mud-bank with two bedraggled, skeeter-bumpy gator grabbers sitting bleakly inside; while outside a great herd of gators grunted and bumped their snouts curiously against the bars.

They came out of the primordial slough, out of the log litters and pin-downs and palmettos. They came by dozens, hundreds—long ones, short ones, great mossy granddaddies, big burly bulls, and the mama, gators with all their spidery-legged tads. Gators, gators, gators, all blinking and staring at the two strange men in the cage.

"Y'know," the younger gator grabber said, "hit 'pears to me thet somethin's gone an' got a mite twisted. We was goan have Shovel Nose in this here cage so as tourist-type folk could come see him. Now why is hit thet we be inside the blame cage with gators comin' to see us?"

"Oh shet yer biggity mouth, cain't you?" the older gator grabber mumbled.

ABOUT THE AUTHOR

ROBERT EDMOND ALTER (1925–1965) wrote with equal facility about gators and gator grabbers, Indian fighters, and thirteenth-century Saxons and Normans. Bob Alter decided at the age of sixteen to be a social worker. He became, instead, a citrus picker, a movie extra, and a soldier. In his early 1930s he began to write, soon publishing a steady string of adult novels, juvenile novels, non-fiction books, and a hundreds of stories in such magazines as *Saturday Evening Post*, *Argosy*, *Alfred Hitchcock's Mystery Magazine*, and *Boys' Life*.

CPSIA information can be obtained
at www.ICGtesting.com
Printed in the USA
LVHW040718280519
619258LV00001B/206/P